one white dolphin

one white dolphin

written by **gill lewis**

illustrated by **RAQUEL APARICIO**

Atheneum Books for Young Readers
New York   London   Toronto   Sydney   New Delhi

ATHENEUM BOOKS FOR YOUNG READERS
An imprint of Simon & Schuster Children's Publishing Division
1230 Avenue of the Americas, New York, New York 10020
For information about special discounts for bulk purchases, please
contact Simon & Schuster Special Sales at 1-866-506-1949 or business@
simonandschuster.com.
The Simon & Schuster Speakers Bureau can bring authors to your live
event. For more information or to book an event, contact the Simon &
Schuster Speakers Bureau at 1-866-248-3049 or visit our website at
www.simonspeakers.com.
Book design by Sonia Chaghatzbanian
The text for this book is set in Garamond.
The illustrations for this book are rendered in India ink and liquid pencil
on Bristol board and watercolor paper.
Manufactured in the United States of America
0512 FFG
First Edition
10 9 8 7 6 5 4 3 2 1
Library of Congress Cataloging-in-Publication Data
Lewis, Gill.
One white dolphin / Gill Lewis ; illustrated by Raquel Aparicio.
p. cm.
Summary: When a baby albino dolphin caught in old fishing netting
washes ashore, Paralympics sailing hopeful Felix and English school
girl Kara work with veterinarians and specialists to save and reunite the
dolphin with her mother, setting off a chain of events that might just
save the reef from the environmental effects of proposed dredging.
ISBN 978-1-4424-1447-1 (hardcover)
ISBN 978-1-4424-1450-1 (eBook)
[1. Dolphins—Fiction. 2. Wildlife rescue—Fiction. 3. Seashore—Fiction.
4. Marine ecology—Fiction. 5. Ecology—Fiction. 6. Environmental
protection—Fiction. 7. England—Fiction.] I. Aparicio, Raquel, ill.
II. Title.
PZ7.L5865On 2012
[Fic]—dc23   2012009182

To Mum and Dad
and
the Nerys Jane
—G. L.

one white dolphin

prologue

Each night it is the same. I stand here on the shoreline, curling my toes into cool, wet sand. Above, the moon is bright, bright white. It spills light, like a trail of milk upon the water. The dolphin is here again, her pearl-white body curving through the midnight sea. She twists and turns beyond the breaking waves, willing me to follow. But the ocean is vast and black, and I don't know what lies beyond this shore. So I just stand and watch her swim away.

Each night I have this dream. Each night the white dolphin waits for me. But where she goes, I am too afraid to follow.

1

I rip another page from the book.

I tear it out, right out.

The paper is tissue thin and edged with gold. It flutters in my hand like a tiny bird, desperate to escape. I let it go and watch it fly up into the clear, blue sky.

I rip out another, and another. The pages soar and tumble across cow-scattered fields into the haze above the silver blue sea.

"Oi, Kara!"

I look down. Jake's pink face is squinting up at me against the glare of sun. Ethan's standing next to him, trying to find fingerholds in the granite blocks of the wall. He jumps to pull me off, but I pull my legs up out of reach.

The wall's too high.

I'm safe up here.

"Kara-Two-Planks!" yells Jake. "Teacher's looking for you."

I run my finger along the rough leather binding of the book. It's heavy in my lap. The hard edges dig into my skin. I rip out another page and set it free, soaring upward, skyward.

"You're in big trouble, Kara-Two-Planks!" shouts Jake. "That Bible is school property. You'll be sent to hell for that."

"She won't get there, though," calls Ethan. "She won't be able to read the signs."

Jake laughs. "Learn to spell your name yet, Kara? K-a-r-a W-o-o-d. Kara-Thick-as-Two-Planks-of-Wood."

I've heard all this before, a thousand times. I turn my back on them and look down to the footpath on the far side of the wall. It runs one way to the coast path along the cliffs, and the other, down steps tangled with nettles and bindweed to the harbor in the town below.

"What I want to know," says Ethan, "is Kara Wood as thick as her dad?"

"My mum says," confides Jake, "that Kara's dad lost his last job because he couldn't write his own name."

Ethan sniggers.

I spin around and glare at them. "Shut up about my dad."

But Jake's not finished. "I heard your mum had to write his name for him. Isn't that right, Kara?"

My eyes burn hot with tears.

"Who writes his name for him now, Kara?"

I blink hard and turn back to the sea. The waves out there are tipped with white. I feel the hot sun on my face. I mustn't cry. I won't let them see me cry.

If I ignore them, they'll go away like they always do. The sea breeze is damp and salty. It catches the white cotton of my shirt and billows it out like a spinnaker sail. I close my eyes and imagine I am sailing across an endless sea, a wide, blue ocean, with nothing else around me but the sun and wind and sky.

"Oi, Kara!"

Jake's still there.

"It's a shame about the Merry Mermaid!" he shouts.

If Jake knows about the Merry Mermaid, then everyone does.

I turn around to look at him.

A few other children from class are watching us from a distance. Chloe and Ella are both looking this way from under the deep shade of the horse chestnut tree. Adam has stopped his game, his soccer ball clutched against his chest.

"Still," Jake says, "it never was much of a pub. It'll make a great holiday home for someone, a rich Londoner probably. I heard the food was terrible."

Jake knows my dad works in the kitchens of the

Merry Mermaid. He knows he'll have no job and no money to live on when it closes at the end of the summer. Jake would love it if we had to move from Cornwall.

"Maybe your dad can come back and work for mine on our trawlers?" says Jake. "Tell your dad we'll be fishing for shellfish when the dredging ban is lifted in ten days' time. Dad's even bought new gear to rake every corner of the seabed out there. He can't wait."

I just glare at him.

Jake laughs. "I'll ask him if you can come too."

I tighten my grip on the Bible's hard leather binding.

Beyond, I see Mrs. Carter striding toward us. I could try and hide the book, but Jake and Ethan would tell her anyway.

"Have you seen the advertisement at the boatyard, Kara?" asks Jake. He's looking at me now and grinning. Ethan's grinning too. They know something I don't. It's in Jake's voice, and he's bursting to tell me.

Mrs. Carter's halfway across the playground. Her face is set and grim.

"The *Moana*'s up for sale!" Jake shouts out. He's jubilant now.

I scramble to my feet. "Liar!"

It can't be true. I'm sure it can't.

But Jake is smug. He pulls his trump card. "My dad's going to buy her and chop her up for firewood!" he shouts. "'Cause he says that's all she's good for."

I hurl the book at him. The Bible's hard edge slams into Jake's nose and he drops like a stone, both hands clutched across his face.

Mrs. Carter is running now. "Kara!"

I glance down at Jake, moaning in the dirt below me.

"Kara, come down now!" Mrs. Carter yells.

But I turn away from them all and jump, leaving Jake Evans bleeding through his fat fingers, turning the dust-dry ground blood red.

I run and run, down the nettled footpath, along cobbled lanes and back alleyways to the sea front. I have to find Dad.

I have to.

The town is busy, clogged with traffic and the sound of drills and diggers working on the new road into the harbor. Beyond the traffic cones and construction fences sits the Merry Mermaid, her roof green with weathered thatch. The air is thick with the smell of beer and chips. The tables sprawled across the pavement are packed with people eating lunch in summer sunshine. The Merry Mermaid scowls down at them from her faded painted sign above the door. I slip through into the darkness and let my eyes adjust from the glare outside.

"You okay, Kara?" Ted is polishing a glass in his hand, turning its rim around and around with a cloth.

"I'm fine," I say. "Where's Dad?"

"He took the day off," he says. He holds the glass up to the light, inspecting it for smudges. "Is everything all right, Kara? He didn't seem himself today."

I look around, as if I expect Dad still to be here.

Ted puts the glass down and leans on the bar toward me. "You sure you're okay?"

"Yes," I say. "I'm fine."

I back out of the pub. The sun is bright. It

shimmers off the whitewashed houses. I start running away from the harbor and up the hill to the new estate on the other side of town. A stitch stabs into my side, but I keep running past front gardens and driveways, past scraps of green with wading pools and tricycles and on to the end house, where a trailer sits on bricks upon the grass.

I slow down and push open the front gate. Aunt Bev is hanging overalls and oilskins on a washing line strung between the garage and the trailer. Uncle Tom must be back from sea.

Aunt Bev pulls back the legs of the overalls to look at me and rests her hand on her swollen belly. She holds two wooden clothes-pegs in her teeth. They stick out like warthog tusks.

I try the handle of the trailer door. Flakes of red rust crumble from the door frame, but the door is locked. "Where's Dad?" I ask.

Aunt Bev takes the pegs out of her mouth. "You should be at school," she says.

I hammer on the trailer door.

"Your dad went out," she says.

I try the door again.

"I said he went *out*." Aunt Bev pegs a pair of trousers to the line. She doesn't take her eyes off me.

I duck under the line and try to dash past into the kitchen to her house, but she puts her hand across the door.

"You in trouble, Kara?" she asks.

"Forgotten something, Auntie Bev," I say. "That's all."

"Well, be quick," she says. "Uncle Tom's asleep. Don't wake him." She lifts a hand from the doorway and lets me pass.

I feel her watching me climb the stairs and slip into the room I share with Daisy. Daisy's sitting on her bed among her dolls, reading Teddy-Cat one of her fairy books. She stuffs something behind her back as I come in. I hear it rustle in her hand. A tell-tale marshmallow lies upon her princess-pink duvet.

"You're home from school," I say. "You're meant to be ill."

Daisy's mouth is full. She looks at the open door and then at me.

I smile. "Don't worry. I won't tell."

A blob of sticky dribble slides down her chin. "I feel sick now," she says.

"I'm not surprised," I say. I wipe the sugar dust from the bed and sit down beside her. "Daisy, have you seen my dad?"

Daisy nods. "Uncle Jim's gone fishing," she says. "He took his poles, them long ones." Her hair bounces as she nods. It's light and frizzy, a sign the good weather's set to stay. I've seen it go tight and curly before the storms blow in.

"How long ago?"

"Not long," she says. "Just after Mum had her coffee."

"Thanks, Daisy." I reach under my cot for my swimming bag, mask, and flippers. Daisy's toys are scattered on my bed. A pink marshmallow is pressed into my pillow. I can't complain, really. It's her room after all. And they'll need my space when the baby comes.

"Are you going with him?" Daisy asks.

I nod. "Please don't tell."

Daisy draws her fingers across her heart and presses them against her lips.

I change into T-shirt and shorts, and it's not until I hear a door slam and voices on the drive outside that I realize a car has pulled up outside the house. Jake's dad's big, black pickup is parked across the drive. I back away from the window. I don't want Jake's dad to see me here.

I hear him talking to Aunt Bev in the kitchen.

"Jim's not up there, Dougie." Aunt Bev's voice is high and tight. "I'll get him to call when he gets back."

"It's his girl I want to see."

"Kara?" Aunt Bev says. I hear her hesitate and stumble on the words. "She's at school."

Through the crack in the bedroom door, I see

Aunt Bev below me in the hallway. She's blocking the doorway to the kitchen. The back of her neck is bright scarlet and she twists a tea towel round and round her hands.

Dougie Evans leans his hand on the door frame. "I know she's up there, Bev."

Aunt Bev takes a step back. Her voice is quiet, almost a whisper. "What d'you want with her?"

"Just a word, that's all."

"What's she done?"

Dougie Evans is in the hallway now, at the foot of the stairs, his sea boots on Aunt Bev's clean carpet. "She broke Jake's nose, that's what she's done."

I close the door and press myself against it.

Feet sound on the stairs, loud and heavy.

Daisy stares wide-eyed at me, the duvet pulled up around her chin. "He's coming up," she whispers.

I push the cot up against the door and cross the room to the window. The garage roof below is flat, but it's still a long way down.

"Kara!" It's Aunt Bev calling now. Her voice is

singsong, almost casual, but I can hear the tremor in it. "Dougie Evans wants to see you."

I throw my bag down to the garden and swing my legs out of the window.

Knuckles rap against the door. It flies open and jams against the cot.

Dougie shouts through the gap. "Kara, let us in!"

"Go," mouths Daisy.

I drop onto the roof, twisting as I land. From there I jump down to soft grass. I turn and see Dougie Evans, red-faced and leaning from the window. But he can't stop me now.

No one can.

I grab my bag and run.

One White Dolphin

15

3

"Wait!" I yell. "Wait!"

I see *Moana* before I see Dad. She looks small compared to other boats in the harbor. With her terra-cotta-colored sails and open wooden deck, she stands out from the molded whiteness of the modern yachts. I scramble down steps and run along the dock, my feet thudding on the boards. *Moana* is drifting slowly out toward the narrow gap between the high harbor walls. I see Dad sitting at the tiller.

"Dad!" I shout. "Wait for me."

Dad pushes the tiller across and *Moana*'s sails flap loose as she turns back into the wind. She drifts toward me, her painted hull throwing rippled patterns of pale blue upon the water. She could have sailed out from one of the old photos of this harbor from a hundred years ago.

I steady myself as she bumps against the dock, grab the mooring rope, and pull her in. "Take me with you," I say.

Dad shades his eyes against the sun to look at me. "Why aren't you at school?"

"I can't stay at school," I say. "Not today, of all days, Dad."

Dad just sits there, one hand on the tiller, watching me. I wonder if he remembers today, if it means something to him too. *Moana*'s sails flap and ruffle above our heads. She's impatient to be off.

"Let me come, Dad," I say. I want to ask him if it's true about *Moana*, if he's really going to sell her. But something stops me, because I want to sail her

17

one last time, not knowing if it's true. It's safe not knowing. It leaves a small space inside for hope.

Dad rubs the stubble on his chin. "All right." He sighs. "Get in."

I climb onboard, pull my life jacket on, and push *Moana* away. The water here behind the long arms of the harbor walls is deep and green and still. Rainbow ripples of oil spread out across its surface. Dad sets the mainsail and I pull in the jib. I watch the triangle of sail above me pull taut and catch the wind, and we slide under the shadow of the harbor and out to sea.

The sea is alive out in the bay. A steady offshore breeze is blowing, kicking up small waves flecked with tips of white. Salt spray flies over *Moana*'s bow as she dips and rises out toward the headland. I sit and watch the harbor town and the pale strip of golden sand slip far into the distance. The school and Aunt Bev's house are soon lost among the sprawl of roads and houses that rise above the harbor. The yachts and trawlers in the harbor and the long, white roof of the fish market seem far away now, too; another world away almost.

And it is just us, again.

Moana, Dad, and me.

I sit beside Dad, but he doesn't look at me. His eyes are focused on the distant horizon, looking beyond there somehow, to another place that I can't see. He could almost be sailing in a different boat, on some different sea. I close my eyes and try to think back to how it used to be.

Beyond the headland, the wind is strong and cold. It blows in from the west, gusting dark ruffles on the water. I wish now that I'd thought to grab a sweater and put on jeans instead. I wrap my arms around my knees and watch goose pimples rise on my arms and legs.

"You okay, Kara?"

I look up and see Dad watching me now. I nod, but my teeth still chatter.

"Get your blanket if you're cold," he says.

I slide forward on the seats and open the small

locker under the foredeck. Three blankets are neatly folded where they always are, strapped to the low shelf above the tool kit and the flares. I pull my blanket out and wrap it around me. It's deep turquoise, like the summer sea, woven through with strips of silver ribbon.

I curl up against *Moana*'s curves and bury my head in the thick folds of blanket, breathing in the salty mustiness of it. The ocean rushes beneath us, a constant stream of white noise. Waves slap against *Moana*'s hull, like a heartbeat. I touch the painted wood to feel it pulse against my hand. Somewhere under the thick layers of paint are the pencil drawings of leaping dolphins that Mum drew for me. I try to trace the outline of them with my fingers now. I can almost smell the sawdust and steamed wood of the boat shed where Mum and Dad rebuilt *Moana*. If I close my eyes, I can still see Dad curving steamed planks of wood to make *Moana*'s hull, Mum laying white caulk between the boards to make her watertight, and me sitting in the dirt, floating paper boats across wide puddle seas.

Mum, Dad, and me.

Those pencil dolphins are still there beneath the paint, etched into *Moana*'s hull. I try to picture them in my mind. I never thought I would forget, but somehow, now, it seems that however hard I try, I just can't see them anymore.

And it must be like this that I fall asleep, cradled in *Moana*'s hull. Because when I wake, the wind has dropped and *Moana* is still. Her sails are down and she is rocking gently, anchored in the shelter of the cove where we keep our lobster traps. Threads of hot, sweet coffee steam drift my way from Dad's red tin cup. The sun is warm on my back, and the sea is turquoise blue, rippled with silver light. Somewhere above a seagull cries. But otherwise, all is quiet and still.

Dad is leaning over the side, pulling on rope. It coils in the boat, dripping seaweed and seawater. He hoists a lobster trap in and places it on the floor. I can see a tangle of legs and antennae of a lobster inside. It's a big one and will fetch a good price at market. I know we need the money.

Dad opens the trap and runs his hand along the armored shell of the lobster's back. He draws it out, and its claws slash through the air. Its red antennae flick backward and forward. Dad turns it over, and in the soft protected curve of its belly lie hundreds of tiny eggs bunched together, glistening black in the sunlight.

"She's berried," I say. "We can't sell her. Look at all those eggs."

Dad looks up. He's just noticed I'm awake. "We'll take her and release her in the marine reserve," he says.

"Not much point," I say. I scowl at him. "Jake says his dad is going to pull his dredging chains across every last corner of the reserve when the dredging ban is lifted."

Dad places the lobster in a large black bucket and covers it with a towel. His face is tight in a frown, running deep creases across his face. He knows there's nothing we can do to stop Dougie Evans from destroying the reef.

"Keep out of Jake's way," he says. "He's got a nose for trouble, like his dad."

I stifle a laugh. I picture Jake lying in the dirt, blood pouring down his face. "Not anymore he hasn't."

Dad looks up. I try to hide my smile, but I can tell Dad's seen already.

"You in trouble, Kara?" asks Dad.

I lift the towel and peer in at the lobster. She glares at me with her small black eyes. "She needs seawater in there," I say.

"What else has Jake been saying?" asks Dad.

I cover the bucket with the towel and sit back, so I can look Dad in the eyes. I ask the question that has filled my mind all this way. "Is *Moana* up for sale?"

Dad turns away. I watch as he ties a chunk of mackerel bait for the lobster trap, and throws it back into the water. The coil of rope unwinds and disappears into the wavering shafts of light.

"It's true, isn't it?" I say. "You're selling her. You're selling *Moana*."

I want him to tell me that it's not true, because Dad never lies to me.

But he doesn't say that.

He turns to look at me. "Yes," he says. "It's true."

And that's all he says. But it's like the breath has been punched right out of me.

"But you can't," I say. It comes out in barely a whisper.

"We've got no choice, Kara," he says. "I owe more money than I'll ever earn. We can't even afford her mooring fee."

I twist the end of my blanket around and around in my hand. "What about Mum?" I mumble the words.

Dad flicks the last drops of his coffee out to sea and screws on the thermos's cap tight. "There's no other way."

"What about Mum?" I say it louder this time, to make sure he can hear me.

"Mum's gone," he says. He looks right at me. "She's been gone a year today. D'you think I don't know that? She's gone, Kara. It's just us now."

I stare at him. Dad hasn't talked about Mum for

months. "Mum would never sell *Moana*," I say. "She belongs to all of us. We built her together. How will you tell Mum you sold *Moana* when she comes back? She'll come back; I know she will."

Dad watches me, like he's trying to decide just what to say.

"She'll send a sign," I say. My eyes are blurred with tears. I blink and push them back. I think of the dove feather I found the day Mum disappeared. I think of the cowrie shell, pure white; the one I found by candlelight, the night we floated candles for her out to sea. "Like she did before, she'll send a sign."

Dad holds me by my shoulders, but his hands are trembling. "Let it go, Kara," he says. "There are no signs. There never were."

I push Dad's hands away.

The silence is thick between us.

The wind is still. The water flat, like glass.

"Kara," Dad says. He kneels down in front of me. "Look at me."

I close my eyes tight.

"Kara . . ."

I cover my ears because I don't want to listen.

I fold my head into my lap to block him out.

I don't want to hear what he's going to say.

I don't want to hear it.

But it's no use.

I hear him say it anyway.

"Mum is *never* coming back."

4

Dad has never said those words before. I stand up and back away from him.

"You've given up," I say. "You've given up."

"Kara . . ."

I pull off my life jacket and reach into my bag for my face-mask and fins.

"Kara, sit down," says Dad.

I push my feet into my fins, pull on my face-mask, and stand up on *Moana*'s side, holding onto the metal shrouds that support her mast. The water below is crystal clear.

"Kara, come down . . ." Dad reaches out his hand.

But I don't take it.

I let go of the shrouds and dive into the water, down into bright blueness shot with sunlight. I turn and watch a trail of silver bubbles spiral upward. I see Dad through the rippled surface, leaning out, looking down. I kick my fins hard and pull through the water, swimming away from him and toward the shore.

I count the seconds in my head before I can burst above the water. I count the seconds before I let myself breathe. My heart is pounding fast, too fast. I can't relax. My lungs burn. My ribs ache. I can't find the quiet space in my head that lets my heart slow down and my mind go clear. I'm too angry for that. I have to breathe. I burst upward and gulp the air.

I'm halfway between Dad and the shore. I can hear Dad call my name, but I keep swimming until my hands touch the soft sand of the cove. I pull my fins and mask off and walk barefoot up through the rocks to the clifftop path. My T-shirt flaps wet and cold against me, and my shorts cling to my legs, but I keep walking and don't look back.

It's only when I reach the stile that turns inland, that I double back and crawl through the long grasses. *Moana*'s sails are up, and Dad is sailing from the small cove. I watch *Moana* sail toward the marine reserve, the stretch of seabed that lies between the shore and Gull Rock, a mile out to sea. *Moana*'s sails cast long shadows in the early evening sun.

I sit up and brush the sand and sea salt from my clothes, and look around. A fresh breeze ripples through the grasses. There's no one else up here, just me. I don't want to go back to Aunt Bev's house. I can't face her and Uncle Tom. I don't want to face Dad now either.

Beyond this cove there is another smaller cove, too narrow for most boats to enter. The water is deep and crystal clear. It shelves up to a strip of sandy beach. I head there now, away from the coastal path, toward the green wall of gorse that lines these cliffs. The gorse spikes snag my T-shirt as I scramble between the bushes to the cliff's edge. Below the crumbly topsoil and twisted roots of gorse, a ledge of hard, dark rock cuts through the softer green-gray layers of slate, and curves down to the cove. I climb down, finding all the footholds and handholds I know so well, counting the layers of folded rock. Millions and millions of years squashed together. Like explorers going back in time, Mum used to say.

The small beach is covered by the high tide. I edge my way to the flat rocks that jut out beyond the cove and into the sea. Sometimes grey seals haul out on these rocks and lie basking in the sun. I press my back into a hollow curve of a rock worn eggshell-smooth by wind and waves.

Mum used to sit here with me, and we'd watch for dolphins. I used to think she had special powers, as if she could feel them somehow or hear them calling through the water. Sometimes we'd wait for hours. But she always knew they'd come. They would rise up like magical creatures from another world, the sunlight shining from their backs, the sound of their breaths bursting above the water. They would leap and somersault in the water, just for us it seemed. It made me feel as if we'd been chosen somehow, as if they wanted to give us a glimpse of their world too.

I haven't been back here since then. Not since Mum left. I wrap my arms around my knees and stare out across the gold, flat sea. The sun's rim touches the horizon, bleeding light into the water. I've been waiting for a sign from Mum all day, but it's too late now. The sun has almost set.

Maybe Dad is right and there are no signs to look for.

Maybe I have to accept that Mum is never coming back.

I watch the last rays of sunshine flare, like beacons across the sky.

And then I see it.

I see a flash of white leap from the water.

The light shines on its smooth curved body before it plunges back into the sea.

I scramble to my feet and stand at the ocean's edge, watching the spread of golden ripples.

This is the sign I have been waiting for.

I just know it is.

It has to be.

The dolphin leaps into the air again. It's white, pure white. It twists and somersaults before diving underwater, sending up plumes of golden spray.

I see other dolphins, too, their gray streamlined bodies and dorsal fins curving through the water. There must be at least fifty dolphins, a huge pod of them. I've never seen so many at one time. Their bursts of breath blast through the stillness.

But it's the white dolphin I'm looking for. Then I see it again, much smaller than the rest. Its pale body is tinged with pink and gold in the fading light. A much larger dolphin swims close by its side.

One White Dolphin

33

Mother and calf, they break the surface together with perfect timing. I watch them swim side by side, out into the open sea. I wrap my arms around me and feel warm, despite the chill night air. I feel so close to Mum somehow, as if she's right here beside me, as if she sent the dolphins. I can almost see Mum's face, her big, wide smile. I can't help wondering if, wherever she is right now, she is thinking of me too.

I watch the dolphins until I can no longer see their fins trail dark lines upon the water. The sea has darkened under a star-scattered indigo sky. The silhouettes of two oystercatchers skim across the surface, their short pointed wings beating fast and hard. But that is all.

I know Dad will expect me home by now. I scramble up the cliff to the coastal path that runs between the cliff's edge and the fields. The air is fresh and damp with dew. It clings in a pale mist above the wheat fields that run inland. The in-between light of dusk holds everything in a strange stillness, like time's drawn breath.

And it feels to me as if *everything* is about to change.

5

The tarmac of the coast road is still warm from the day's sun. It's more than two miles home from here, and I hope Dad's not waiting for me. He has a late shift at the pub today, so maybe I can slip back without him noticing.

I haven't walked far along the road before a car pulls up, its headlights glaring in my eyes.

The passenger window slides down. "KARA! Is that you?"

It's Aunt Bev. She leans across from the driver's side. She's furious. I wish I'd walked across the fields back home instead.

"What's wrong?" I say.

"Just get in the car, Kara," she snaps. "Now."

I climb into the backseat next to Daisy. She's in her dressing gown and slippers, munching a family-size bag of crisps. She's usually in bed by now.

Aunt Bev twists round to glare at me. "What's wrong?" She spits the words out.

I glance at Daisy. She points at me and draws her hand across her throat. I'm as good as dead.

"What's wrong?" shouts Aunt Bev again. "The coast guard and the police are out looking for you, that's what's wrong. Your dad's in a right state. He's gone with them too." She slams the car into gear and we lurch forward. "You've got some questions to answer when we get back. I can tell you that, my girl."

I say nothing. I strap up my seat belt and say nothing.

We drive back home in silence and in darkness. Daisy takes my hand into hers and squeezes it. I squeeze hers back.

"I told them you'd be okay," she whispers. "But they wouldn't listen."

"That's enough from you, Daisy," snaps Aunt Bev. "You should've been in bed an hour ago."

Back at the house I sit in the kitchen and wait for Dad. I can hear Uncle Tom phoning the police and coast guard to say that I've been found. Aunt Bev is heating up a pan of milk for Daisy's bedtime drink. Daisy's been told to go upstairs, but she's sitting at the kitchen table, twirling a curl of golden hair around and around her finger.

She leans across so our heads are close together. "What happened?"

The question catches me off guard.

"The white dolphin came," I whisper.

Daisy's eyes open wide. She's the only one who knows about the dreams I have.

"It's bedtime for you, Daisy," says Aunt Bev. She

pours the warm milk into a mug and points up the stairs.

I stand up to go too, but Aunt Bev signals me to stay. I don't want to be here, just her and me. I watch Daisy cup her hands around her mug and leave the room. She gives a small smile before disappearing around the door and up the stairs.

Aunt Bev pours herself a mug of tea and leans against the oven. "Well?" she says.

I stare at my hands and say nothing.

"I heard you busted Jake Evans's nose today."

I look up at her. She's glaring at me, daring me to challenge her.

I don't deny it.

"The only person with a proper job in this house is employed by Jake's dad," she snaps. "Do you want Uncle Tom to lose his job as well? Do you?"

I shake my head. "No, Auntie Bev," I say. "I'm sorry."

She sighs and rubs her hand across her swollen belly. "God knows this year's been hard for you,

Kara, but you're not the only one who's struggling. We can't go on like this. It's time we had some straight talking in this family. . . ."

But she doesn't finish because Dad bursts through the door.

He pushes past the table and pulls me into him. He wraps his arms around me, so I'm buried in his thick wool sweater. It smells of wood smoke and engine oil. I feel his warm breath in my hair, and I feel five years old again.

"I'm sorry, Kara," he says. "I'm so sorry."

Aunt Bev's voice cuts through. "It's Kara who should be sorry. She's had us all worried sick."

But Dad holds me by my shoulders. "I'm sorry," he says, "for what I said about Mum. I shouldn't have." His eyes are red, so I could almost think he's been crying, but I've never seen him cry before.

I smile at him. "It going to be okay, Dad. She sent a sign. I saw a dolphin, a white dolphin. Mum sent it for us."

Dad pushes back my hair. He looks right into my

eyes, but I can't tell what he's thinking anymore.

"Mum's still here for us, Dad," I say. "I know she is."

Aunt Bev thumps her mug down, slopping tea across the table. "Your mother stopped being here for you the day she left."

Uncle Tom lays a hand upon her arm. "That's enough, Bev."

Aunt Bev's not finished. "But it's true. And we were left to pick up the pieces. It can't go on like this, Jim. How long are you going to wait for her? Another year? Five years? Ten years?"

"Leave it, Bev." Uncle Tom tries to steer her away. "Not now, not tonight."

Aunt Bev pulls away and glares at Dad. "Kay should never have left. Her responsibilities were *here*." She raps her finger hard on the table to make her point.

Dad sits down and puts his head in his hands. "We've been through this before, Bev. She had her reasons."

"Going halfway around the world on some hippie dolphin-saving trip?" she snaps. "Was that a good enough reason to leave a husband and child?"

I scowl at Aunt Bev. "Mum's a marine biologist!" I shout. "She is stopping people from catching wild dolphins. You *know* that."

But Aunt Bev ignores me and sits down next to Dad. "You've got to face it, Jim. If your own sister can't tell you, then who can? You've just got to accept that Kay isn't coming back."

Dad shoots her a look. "We don't know that, Bev. We just don't know."

Aunt Bev throws her hands up in the air. "Exactly. That's always been the problem. We don't know anything. A year on and still the only thing we *do* know is that she landed in the Solomon Islands, checked into her hotel room . . . and vanished."

Dad shakes his head. "I should have gone and looked for her at the time."

"You couldn't afford the bus fare to the airport, let alone the plane ticket," Aunt Bev snorts. "The authorities couldn't find her. Not even the private detective hired by the families of the others who disappeared could find her. The case is closed."

Dad frowns. "People don't just disappear."

Aunt Bev sits back and looks at Dad. "You can't bury your head in the sand forever, for Kara's sake at least. You've got all Kay's debts to pay. Thousands for that trip and all that fancy diving stuff she bought. But I bet you haven't told Kara that, have you, Jim?"

Dad stands up. His chair knocks back against the wall. "I'm going out."

Uncle Tom shifts aside to let him pass.

"That's right!" Aunt Bev shouts after Dad. "Walk away like you always do."

I stand up too. "Mum wouldn't leave us. I know she'll come back. She sent the dolphin."

Dad stops, his hand on the door.

Aunt Bev glares at Dad's back. "You've got no house, Jim Wood. You'll be out of a job in weeks, and soon no boat." She takes a deep breath and turns to me. "So there'll be no more talk of dolphins in this house, Kara. Is that understood?"

She folds her arms.

She's said her piece.

She's done.

But I don't care. The white dolphin is a sign that Mum's out there somewhere, and I'll wait for her, however long it takes. I want Dad to know this too. Mum will come back. I know she will. We'll live on *Moana*, the three of us, and sleep under canvas stretched across the boom. We'll sail away together one day like she always said we would.

Mum, Dad, and me.

The phone rings through the silence.

Uncle Tom answers it and passes it to Dad. "It's for you, Jim."

Dad takes the phone, and I hear him pacing in the hallway. I hear his voice, soft and quiet. He walks back into the kitchen and puts the phone down on the receiver. He opens the back door, leans against the door frame, and lets the cool night air rush in.

Aunt Bev's got her head on one side. "Well . . . who was that?"

Dad's shoulders are slumped. "It's an offer for *Moana*," he says. "A man wants to view her this weekend."

6

I cut Daisy's toast into triangles and push the plate to her side of the table.

She pulls off the crust and looks at me. "Aren't you having any breakfast?"

"Not hungry," I say.

Aunt Bev looks at me from across the top of her magazine. "You're not having a day off school. The head teacher wants to see you about what you did to Jake Evans's nose."

I frown. I don't want to go to school at all.

"I sent a big box of chocolates to Jake with your name on it," she says. "Cost me nearly ten pounds it did. Let's just hope it keeps his dad happy too."

I get up from the table and grab my schoolbag. "I'll be waiting outside," I tell Daisy.

Outside the sky is clear and blue. A rag of pale gray cloud stretches along the distant horizon above the sea. All I want to do is go out on *Moana*, but Dad left early to cook breakfasts for guests staying at the pub. I lean against the trailer and scuff the dry ground with my feet and wait for Daisy. I wish I was back at the grade school with her too. I felt safe there. It wasn't just words and numbers like it is now in middle school. Mum was still here last year too.

"I'm coming," calls Daisy.

I watch her walk down the path with her schoolbag across her shoulder and a larger bag dragging along the ground. "What've you got in there?" I ask.

"Fairy dress and wings and wand and a present

for Lauren." She grins. "It's her party after school."

I roll my eyes. "I forgot," I say. "Come on, I'll carry it."

I walk Daisy through the mothers and pushchairs at the school gates of the grade school and give her a hug. "I'll be back here after school," I say.

Daisy reaches into her bag and pulls a scrunched-up piece of paper from the pocket. "I did this for you," she says, "for good luck when you see Mrs. Carter."

I flatten the paper out and smile. A white wax-crayon dolphin is swimming in an ink-blue sea. "Thanks, Daisy," I say. "It's just what I need."

I mean it too. I'm going to need all the luck I can get.

I have to miss double art on Friday mornings to have extra sessions with Mrs. Baker, my learning support teacher. I wish I could miss math or computer class instead. Art is the only subject I enjoy. It's not that I mind Mrs. Baker. At least I don't get laughed at in her lessons. She says my dyslexia is just a different way of thinking. I remember her saying it often runs in families, and I reckon that's why Dad can't read or write. Mum once tried to get him to see someone about it, but he wouldn't go; said it was too late for him to learn.

The only spare classroom is a modular building at the far end of the playground, now used as a store. I sit at one of the tables, a tray of sand in front of me. We're doing Mrs. Baker's new technique. Multisensory development, she calls it.

I call it a waste of time.

I pull the tray toward me and pick up a handful of sand, letting the grains run through my fingers. It's the coarse gritty sand from the parking lot end of the beach, not the fine white powder sand near the rock pools toward the headland.

Mrs. Baker pulls up her chair and pats the sand down flat. "Let's try the 'au' sound, as in 'sauce'."

My fingers hover above the sand, and I start to trace the outline of an *a*. I know this one. It's the shape of Gull Rock from the shore, one rounded side and one steep, a dark cave circled in the center. I start the top loop of the *a* where the rocks are stained white with centuries of seabird mess. Gannets nest on the seaward side. I've watched them twist in the air and dive for fish, like white missiles, into the water. Dad and I have seen puffins, too, scoot along above the waves. I curl my finger down to the base where grey seals haul out onto the flat rocks and have their pups on the narrow pebble beach that faces the mainland shore. Submerged rocks and underwater caves and arches spread out into the sea. A wrecked warship has become part of the reef. I run my fingers across in wave patterns in the sand. Mum once showed me a photo she'd taken of a cuckoo wrasse, a fish with bright blue-and-orange markings, swimming through a rusted port-hole, and another of pink-and-white feather stars living along the old gun barrels. The whole reef spreads out from Gull Rock to the shore, an underwater safari park, a hidden wilderness.

"Kara!"

I look up. I didn't hear Mrs. Carter come into the room. She smiles briefly at Mrs. Baker and pulls up a chair beside me. She slides the Bible and some of the ripped pages on the table.

"I think Kara and I need a talk," she says.

Mrs. Baker's eyes flit between us. She gathers up her papers and shoulders her saggy carpetbag. "There's no lesson next Friday, Kara, as it's the last day of term, so if I don't see you before then, have a lovely summer."

I watch her walk out toward the parking lot at the back of the school.

A cloud shadow slides across the playground, darkening the room.

Mrs. Carter leans forward in her chair. "I hear you've been making great improvements with your writing," she says. Her smile is a thin, hard line.

I stare at the tray of sand and run my fingers through the coarse grains. We both know we're not here to talk about my dyslexia today.

"I know this year's been hard for you, Kara."

I look up again. Mrs. Carter is watching me. She takes her glasses off and folds them neatly on the table.

"It's all right to be angry." Her voice is soft, controlled. "I understand."

I trace a circle in the sand, around and around and around. I want this to be over with.

"But you can't take your anger out on other children and school property."

I let silence sit between us.

Mrs. Carter leans closer. "You broke Jake Evans's nose," she says. "How do you feel about that now?"

I dot two eyes and trace the outline of a smile in my circle. "His dad's going to destroy the reef," I say. "He's going to pull his dredging chains across it and rip it up when the ban is lifted."

"There is never an excuse for violence, Kara."

I stare hard at the sand. Mrs. Carter sits back in her seat and folds her arms. I think she wants this to be over with as much as me.

"But why rip up the Bible, Kara? Tell me that."

I want to say it's because she told us God will answer all our prayers. Well, I've been praying for news of Mum for a whole year now, and I haven't heard a thing. But I don't tell her that. Instead, I shrug my shoulders and scrunch the sand up in my hands.

The school bell rings marking the end of the second lesson. The next lesson is math, before the break. I glance up at Mrs. Carter.

"How can we resolve this, Kara?" she asks. "You tell me."

I run my finger along the hard edge of the Bible. Resolve what? Mum not coming back? Dredging the reef? I know she doesn't mean those things at all. I lift the corner of a tissue-thin ripped page. "I could help mend it," I say.

Mrs. Carter sits back in her chair and nods. "It would be a good start," she says. "You can help me repair it on Monday after school. It'll give you the weekend to think things through. But you know I'll have to speak to your father about all this."

I let the sand trickle through my fingers and watch it pile up in a little mountain in the tray.

"And you're to apologize to Jake as well," she says.

I stare at my hands, flecked with tiny crystal grains.

Mrs. Carter stands up and tucks the Bible under her arm. "You can go now."

I stand up and walk away, but I feel her eyes burn in my back. Maybe she can read my mind. I'll help her stick the pages in her Bible.

But I won't say sorry to Jake Evans.

I'd rather die.

7

I stand in silence in the corridor outside the math room door. Through the windows at the end of the hall, I see the bright sunlit playground and far beyond that, the sea. I could walk out of here; just keep walking on and on. There's no one here to stop me, no one here to see. But I don't do that. Instead, I put my hand on the door and push it open. Everyone in my class knows I've had to see Mrs. Carter about breaking Jake Evans's nose. I know they'll all stop and turn and stare when I walk in.

I keep my head down as I walk across the classroom. I stop at the place where I usually sit. But there's someone else already there, in my seat.

"Find another seat, Kara," says Mr. Wilcox above the silence. "Be quick."

I spin around and sit down at a spare desk by the window and spread my math books out in front of me. I glance sideways at the new boy in the class sitting next to Chloe. He's wearing black jeans and a white shirt. But it's his face I notice more. The muscles in his neck stand out in straight, tight lines, pulling the left side of his face down and sideways. It looks like his face has dropped on one side. His left arm is twisted up against his chest and writhes around as if he can't keep it still at all.

He sees me staring, so I look away.

At break, Chloe and Ella stay behind with him to talk to Mr. Wilcox. I guess they've been given the job of showing him around today. They've hardly talked to me at all. No one's mentioned Jake's nose either. I don't think anyone would dare to in front of Jake and Ethan.

It's not until the morning lessons have finished that I can join Chloe and Ella in the lunch queue. I grab a tray and slide it along behind Chloe's.

"Where's that new boy?" I ask.

Chloe looks over her shoulder. "Felix?" she says. "He's only doing mornings. He's just getting to know the school before he joins after the summer."

"It's hardly worth it," I say. "There's only a week left before we break for vacation."

Chloe pours two glasses of water, one for her and one for Ella. "Mrs. Carter said the school might need to make changes before he comes, like put in ramps and hand rails and stuff. He can't walk that well."

"What's he like?" I ask.

Chloe shrugs her shoulders and looks at Ella. "Dunno. Didn't say much, did he?"

"Couldn't wait to go," Ella says. "Don't blame him, though."

Beyond Ella, I see Jake sitting at the table. He's stopped midmouthful to watch us talk. Chloe and Ella have seen him watching too.

I take a plate from the stack. "Daisy can't wait till Lauren's party," I say. "Have you got many coming?"

Chloe puts her plate out for chips. "About fifteen. Mum's dreading it. Dad's just got back from sea, and he's dead tired. Mum wants us to help."

Chloe's dad works with Uncle Tom on Dougie Evans's boats too. He's come home to fifteen Daisys, high on fizzy drinks and birthday cake.

"I don't mind helping too," I say. "I've got to bring Daisy along, anyway."

Chloe glances across at Jake and then at Ella. "We'll be fine," she says. The words come out too quickly. "It'll be a bit crowded in our house. We won't need any help."

Ella stares down at her tray.

"All right," I say. I feel my eyes smart with tears. Chloe and Ella have always let me join in with them before.

"Chips or baked potato?"

I look up. The lunch lady is holding out a scoop of chips in one hand and a baked potato on a fork in the other.

"Chips," I say.

She empties her scoop of chips onto my plate, and I pick up the ones that scatter across my tray.

Chloe slides a chocolate brownie onto her tray and turns to me. "I've got to pick up Lauren and her other friends from school, so I'll take Daisy too," she says.

I nod and pretend to concentrate on the plates of pudding and the bowl of fruit in front of me. "Tell her I'll pick her up at five thirty."

I watch Chloe walk away. She sits down next to Ella on the long table by the window. Jake and Ethan are at the table too. Jake glares at me. His face is a blue-black mess of bruise. A bright white plaster sits across his nose.

I grab an apple and walk across the hall, feeling Jake's eyes on me all the way. The table is full. If Chloe moved up, I could sit next to her, but her back is turned to me and her elbows are spread on either side of her tray. The other tables have older children from eighth and ninth grades. I take my tray and sit at an empty table by the door.

I try to force my lunch down, but my mouth is dry and the chips stick in my throat. I push them to the side, hide them under my knife and fork, and take a bite of apple. It's Friday at least. No school for two whole days and then only one more week until the summer holidays begin.

"Having fun?" Jake puts his empty tray down on the table and sits opposite me. Ethan leans against the door frame and smirks.

I look across at Jake. Close up, one eye is blood-shot red. The edges of the bruise are sickly yellow.

"You don't think you can make up for this with

a box of chocolates, do you?" The corner of Jake's mouth curls up as he speaks.

"It wasn't me who sent them," I say.

I wait for him to go, but he sits there, staring at me.

"You know why my dad hates you so much?" he says.

I stare down at the half-eaten apple on my plate. I know the reason why. I've heard all this before.

Jake leans across the table. "Aaron's dead because of your mum."

I grip the edges of my tray. The fork rattles against the china plate. "Your brother didn't have a life jacket on when he was found," I say.

Jake snorts. "My dad says you're going pay for this." He lowers his voice so not even Ethan can hear. "Soon you and your dad will have *nothing* left."

8

I slip my hand through Daisy's. "Good party?" I ask. Her fairy tutu rustles as we swing arms, and she skips along beside me.

Daisy nods and smiles up at me. "Why didn't you come too?"

I glance back at the house. Lauren's waving from the door, but there's no sign of Chloe or Ella.

"I had to do some shopping for your mum," I lie.

Daisy runs ahead and pulls me by the hand. "Will you play with me at home?"

I shake my head. "I'm going out."

"Where?"

"Just out."

She stops and pulls away from me. "You're going to look for the white dolphin, aren't you?"

I hold my hand out. "Come on, Daisy," I say. "I told Aunt Bev I'd get you home."

It's not entirely true, but I want to go back to the cove, and I can't take Daisy with me.

"I want to come with you," she says. She juts her chin out and just stands there, like she's not going anywhere. A gust of wind blows her long blond curls across her face. Her fairy wings flutter. She clutches her wand and party bag in one hand and folds her arms across her chest.

"Come *on*, Daisy," I say. I'm not in the mood to fight. *"Please."*

She shakes her head. She looks like the sugarplum fairy. Sugar-plump and squashed into a ballet dress, about to have a tantrum.

I sit back on a low wall behind me and rest my head in my hands. I feel we could be here awhile.

"I'll buy you an ice cream at Zagni's," I say. I jangle some coins in my pocket. I hope I've got enough to buy one. Maybe Daisy won't feel like one after all that party food. But I know Daisy. She never turns down an ice cream. I wait and watch.

Daisy twirls her wand around and around. She puts her hands on her hips and looks at me. "It has to be mint chocolate chip," she says.

"Done," I say. "Mint chocolate chip it is."

I get up from the wall, ready to go.

"And M&Ms," says Daisy.

I shake my head. "Haven't got enough money for that."

"Chocolate sauce, then?"

I nod. "You've got yourself a deal."

Daisy flashes her smile at me and takes my hand. Her hand is small and soft and warm, like putty. She skips along beside me, her tiara bouncing on her curls. And I can't help smiling too, because Daisy manages to wrap *everyone* around her little finger.

Zagni's is warm inside. Too warm. Condensation clings to the windows. We stand in the ice cream and pizza queue and wait. The queue is long and snakes around the chairs and tables by the racks of post-cards, shell necklaces, and key rings. We edge forward, and I see Jake and Ethan at one of the tables. I want to leave and go back outside, but Daisy has my hand held tightly in hers. I hide behind the man in front of me and keep my head down, out of sight.

Jake and Ethan haven't seen me. They're watching a boy and a tall fair-haired woman arguing at one of the tables by the window. I can't hear what they're saying, but the woman slams her hands on the table and stands up. Her chair knocks backward to the floor, and she stoops to pick it up. The boy glares at her as she storms past us and out through the door. It's only now that I can clearly see his face.

"He's the new boy," I whisper to Daisy. "He was in my class today."

Felix gulps his drink and leans back in his chair. He wipes his sleeve across his face, leaving a trail of orange juice on his chin.

Daisy tugs my arm. "What's wrong with him?"

"I don't know, Daisy." I pull her arm. "Come on, it's rude to stare."

I hear Jake explode with laughter and look up. But it's not me they're laughing at this time. It's Felix. Ethan pulls his arm up against his chest and pulls a leery grin. Felix's face darkens. He looks across at me, as if I'm in with them too, so I turn away.

We shuffle forward in the queue.

But Jake and Ethan aren't done. I hear them laugh again.

I look around to see Ethan letting a trail of saliva dribble down his chin.

Daisy hangs back on my hand. I try to pull her forward, but she breaks free.

"Stop it!" she yells. "Just stop it." She stands in front of Jake and Ethan, hand on hip, wand raised like Tinker Bell in front of Captain Hook and Smee. She points at Felix. "He can't help it," she says. Her wings bristle and her face glows bright red.

Jake and Ethan snigger. But people in the café are turning in their seats to look at them. Jake stands up, sees me, and scowls. "Come on, Ethan," he says. He shoves past me and mutters under his breath but loud enough for me to hear. "It's just for spastics and losers in here."

Daisy grips my hand again, tighter this time. I can feel her nails dig into my palm.

I put an arm round her and glance back at Felix. He's staring at the table, spinning the salt shaker round and round with his good hand.

We reach the counter, about to order, but Mrs. Zagni has an ice cream ready for Daisy. Two scoops of mint chocolate chip, dripping with chocolate sauce and a chocolate M&Ms.

"This one's on the house, Daisy Varcoe," she said with a smile. "That's a big thing you did back there. You're what the world needs right now."

Daisy beams and takes the ice cream.

"Come on, Daisy." I take her wand and party bag. "Let's get out of here."

"I just want to say hello," she says.

I wait for her by the café door and smile. Daisy wants the whole world to be her friend. She stops in front of Felix's table, puffs out her chest, and grins.

But something happens. Something's said that I can't hear. Daisy's face falls. Tinker Bell's little light has been snuffed out. She drops her ice cream. The cone shatters and splatters mint chocolate chip across the hard tiled floor. Daisy runs right past me, through the open café door, her cheeks burning crimson and streaking with tears.

9

I find Daisy by the harbor. She's sitting between a pile of lobster traps, sobbing and puffing, catching her breath.

"What is it, Daisy? What happened?"

She pulls her wings off and throws them in the dirt. She tries to snap her wand, but the plastic just bends, and she throws that in the mud and oil, too.

"Did you hear what he said?" Her eyes are big and full of tears.

I kneel down and put my arms around her. "What, Daisy?"

She shakes her head and buries her head in my chest.

I lift her chin up. "Come on, Daisy, you can tell me."

"He said . . ." A sob catches in her throat and she gulps it back. "He said . . . he didn't put out an advertisement for a fat fairy godmother."

"You're kidding!" I say.

Daisy shakes her head. "That's what he said."

I try to hide my smile. "Forget it, Daisy. He was rude, that's all."

She looks at me with her big round eyes. "I'm not fat, am I?"

"'Course not," I say, and I smile this time. "You're just right the way you are. And it was a brave thing you did back there."

She looks at me, but she's not convinced. Her face is tearstained and smudged in dirt. Her whole body shudders with big sobs as she breathes.

I lift her to her feet. "Come on. Let's see if we can find that white dolphin."

Her face lights up a little, and she smiles. "Really?"

I nod. I can't take her to the secret cove. The cliffs are too steep to climb, and we won't get back home in time for Aunt Bev.

"Let's go down to the beach," I say. "Maybe we'll see it there."

I take Daisy's hand, and we walk along the beach to the rock pools on the far side. I look out into the sea, but there's no sign of any dolphins in the bay.

"Let's go to the Blue Pool," I say. "Let's see what we can find."

The tide is still low enough for us to pick our way along the slabs of rock and patches of pale sand toward the headland. The rock pools here are deep and hidden. Some are six-foot-wide crevices holding mini–underwater worlds. But there is one rock pool bigger than the rest. It's a mini-universe.

The Blue Pool is a tidal pool, flanked on three sides

by massive slabs of slate. Some fifty years ago, a concrete ledge was built across to keep the water in. It's now a huge, deep rock pool, big enough to swim in. The walls inside are lined with anemones and kelp, and sometimes fish become trapped between the tides.

At high tides, the sea reaches just over the ledge, and then the Blue Pool looks like one of the posh swimming pools I've seen in magazines that go on and on and look like they're part of the sea. It can be packed with people here in high summer. But today it's just Daisy and me.

I take my shoes and socks off and roll my trousers up. I sit down and dip my feet in the cold seawater. I stare down through the sun-bright surface, hoping to see a jellyfish or maybe a large fish trapped inside. "What can you see, Daisy?"

"The Bird Lady," she says in a hushed whisper.

"What?" I ask. I look up. Daisy's pointing along the rocky shore. I didn't see her before. She was hidden in the shadows. But now I see an old lady sitting by the boulders at the water's edge, her long, gray hair and black shawl lifted by the breeze. I watch her tear chunks from a loaf of bread and throw them up into the sky. The gulls wheel and dive to catch them and squabble on the rocks for fallen crumbs.

"It's Miss Penluna," I say. "I thought she'd moved away."

"She's a witch," says Daisy.

"Daisy!" I laugh, because if Miss Penluna had a broomstick, I'd think she was one too.

Daisy frowns at me and folds her arms. "She *is* a witch. Tommy Ansty said when the cows on his dad's farm got big warts, the vet couldn't cure them, but the Bird Lady did. She put a spell on them. Tommy said the warts dropped off the next day."

"Well, watch out," I say. "She's coming this way. She might put a spell on you too."

Daisy tries to pull me up. "Come on, let's go."

"Don't be silly, Daisy," I say. "There's no such thing as witches." Despite my words, I press myself into the rock shadows as she passes. Daisy clings onto me, and we watch her shuffle past and climb the steps worn smooth by people's feet over the years, up to the path along the headland. Her long shawl trails a wet line across the rocks where it's dragged in rock pools on the way. She's almost made it to the top when we see her fall. She stumbles forward. Her walking stick clatters to the ground and slithers down the rocks. All we see is the top of her cloak above the long grasses.

She doesn't move.

I look at Daisy, and Daisy looks at me.

"We'd better check to see if she's okay," I say.

Daisy nods and follows me across the rocks. By the time we reach Miss Penluna, she is sitting up and rubbing both her knees. A small bloodstain has soaked through the ribbing on her woolen tights.

I pick up her stick. "Are you okay?"

Miss Penluna looks up and smiles. "I think so. Thank you, dear."

I hold out my hand. She takes mine in hers, and I help her to her feet. Her arm feels thin and bony beneath her shawl. She's so light, it's as if she's made out of nothing at all. Her birdlike eyes dart across my face.

"You're Kay Wood's child, aren't you?"

The question takes me by surprise. No one talks about Mum anymore.

I nod.

Daisy clutches my hand tight in hers.

"She used to bring me birds," Miss Penluna says. She cups her hands, as if she's holding one. "Funny little black-and-white birds, like penguins. Lost, they were. They couldn't find their rabbit holes in the storm."

I hear Daisy stifle a giggle. She holds her hand across her mouth, and I see the corner of her eyes crinkle in a smile.

But Miss Penluna hasn't noticed. She leans into us, eyes wide, and whispers, "I kept them in my drainpipes for the night."

Daisy is shuddering beside me now, and I cough to hide her helpless giggles. "Are you sure you'll be all right?" I ask.

Miss Penluna nods and pulls her shawl straight around her shoulders. She takes her stick from me. "I'll be just fine now, thank you."

She's about to walk away, but she turns and faces me, her head cocked to one side.

"How is your mother?" she asks. "I haven't seen her since I've been away."

I shrug my shoulders. It's such a simple question, but I don't know the answer anymore. "I don't know where she is," I say.

Miss Penluna's eyes search my face, and I feel careless somehow, like a small child who's lost a precious toy. I thought everyone in this town must have heard about Mum. It was front-page news last year. Four members of one whale and dolphin charity who worked for the Solomon Islands just disappeared, including her. They were helping local people to stop dolphins from being caught for sea-life theme parks around the world. One theme park in Dubai wanted twenty dolphins, and another park in the Caribbean wanted some too. Mum wanted to find out who was behind it all. She said someone was out to make a load of money. *Blood money*, she called it.

Miss Penluna prods me in the chest with her stick. "I'll ask the angels to look for her," she says. "Maybe they can help."

I nod and glance at Daisy. "Thank you." I can't think of anything else to say.

I watch Miss Penluna climb the last few steps and amble slowly along the coastal path back to town.

Daisy turns to me wide-eyed. "Maybe she can find your mum."

"Don't be silly, Daisy," I say. "It's rubbish, all that stuff. She's bonkers. You saw that for yourself."

A gap opens in the clouds and Miss Penluna is lit up in a golden shaft of light, as if it's shining right down from the heavens. I try to push the thought out of my head. It's a stupid thought, I know. But I can't help wondering.

Maybe Miss Penluna can really talk to angels after all.

10

The smell of bacon threads up the stairs and into the room I share with Daisy. She's still asleep, her golden curls spread out across the pillow. I pull my dressing gown on and climb downstairs to the kitchen. Uncle Tom is sitting at the table. He's in his oilskin trousers, and his fishing boots are by the back door. I guess he's going back out to sea today. Aunt Bev is standing at the stove, frying bacon. She rests her other hand on her belly. Her stomach is huge now. The baby is due in six weeks' time.

"Is Daisy up yet?" she asks. She waggles the spatula at me. "I'm taking her to Plymouth with me for the day. I don't want to miss the bus."

"I'll go and see," I say.

I go back up to the bedroom and wake Daisy. She follows me dreamily down the stairs, half-asleep, clutching Teddy-Cat to her chest. Dad is in the kitchen now too, pouring himself a coffee.

"You look smart," I say.

Dad looks up. His hair is brushed and he's wearing his only suit. On Saturday mornings he's usually dressed in his old sweater and jeans, tinkering about with *Moana* at the harbor.

Dad frowns. He nods his head at a light blue folder on the table. "I'm seeing the man who wants to buy *Moana*," he says.

"Don't sign anything till you've let me check the small print," says Uncle Tom. "You want a good price for her."

I sit down and glare at Dad. Daisy sits down next to me and plops Teddy-Cat onto the table.

"Can you move that?" Aunt Bev says. "Can't you see breakfast's ready?"

Daisy pulls Teddy-Cat onto her lap, and Dad puts his folder on the chair beside him. Uncle Tom takes Daisy's plate of bacon and fried eggs and starts cutting up the bacon for her. "Good party last night, Daisy?"

Daisy nods her head and looks at me. "Me and Kara saw the Bird Lady," she says.

Uncle Tom frowns. "The Bird Lady?"

I nod. "Miss Penluna."

"Miss Penluna?" Aunt Bev snorts. She drops another piece of bacon in the pan. "That mad old witch? I'm surprised they let her out."

"Out of where?" I ask.

Uncle Tom coughs and glares at Aunt Bev. "She's not been well," he says.

Daisy leans across the table and whispers, "She says she can talk to angels."

"See what I mean?" says Aunt Bev. The bacon spits and fizzles as she turns up the heat. "She's not changed. Did you know Muriel from the post office once went to see her?"

Uncle Tom shakes his head and takes a glug of coffee.

Aunt Bev lowers her voice. "Muriel wanted to speak to her husband, Ernie, across the other side."

"The other side of where?" asks Daisy.

"Of the grave," says Aunt Bev.

I glance at Daisy. Her eyes are wide, wide open.

Aunt Bev looks around to check she's got all our attention. "Miss Penluna told Muriel she had to bring something of Ernie's to show the angels," she whispers. "Well, Muriel took his pension book along. And do you know what that mad old witch said Ernie's message was?"

Uncle Tom shakes his head.

The clock on the wall ticks through the silence.

Aunt Bev folds her arms across her stomach for greater effect. "She said Ernie wanted to tell Muriel to stop sticking her big nose in everybody's business."

Dad splutters in his coffee.

Uncle Tom hides behind his copy of the *Fishing News*, but I hear him mutter, "Maybe Miss Penluna's not so mad after all."

"That's not even funny," snaps Aunt Bev. "You should have seen the state of Miss Penluna's house when they took her away. Filthy it was. Muriel said there was bird muck everywhere. There were six crows in her living room, for goodness' sake. I'm surprised they didn't burn the house down after she'd gone."

Daisy giggles. "She told us she kept penguins in her drainpipes. She said they couldn't find their rabbit holes in the storm."

Aunt Bev shoves a bit of bacon in her mouth. "See what I mean? Completely mad."

I wash up the dishes while Aunt Bev gets Daisy ready for their trip to Plymouth. They bustle out of the door with bags and coats, and I wave to Daisy as Uncle Tom drives them away to the bus stop at the top of the road leading out of town.

I sit down next to Dad in deep, still silence. It's our space now, for a little while at least.

"Fancy Miss Penluna remembering that," says Dad.

"What?" I ask.

"About the birds," he says. "Mum *did* once take birds to her. Manx Shearwater, they were. Little black-and-white birds that nest in rabbit holes on islands out at sea. And they did look a bit like penguins. Mum found a couple of fledglings that were exhausted after storms had blown them inland." Dad takes a sip of coffee and chuckles. "Miss Penluna kept them in old pieces of drainpipe for the night before she let them go the next day."

I smile. "Maybe Uncle Tom's right," I say. "Maybe Penluna's not as mad as everybody thinks after all."

Dad glances at the clock, lifts the folder from his lap, and puts it on the table. He sighs and runs his hands along the folder's tattered edge. "I'll have to go soon."

I know what's inside the folder. I've seen it countless times before. Dad's shown me the photos of *Moana* when Mum and Dad found her rotting in a creek, photos of her being rebuilt, the drawings and sketches of her design, and a small square patch of sailcloth.

Dad takes one photo out. "I thought we'd keep this one," he says.

I look at it and trace my finger across the top edge. It's the day we launched *Moana*, the first time she had sailed for more than a hundred years. She's supported in a winch frame, about to be lowered into the water. Mum had said our boat needed a new name for a new life. She said it had to be a name to connect us all. So she'd chosen *Moana*, a name from her homeland of New Zealand. In Maori, it means "Ocean."

I tuck the photo into the folder. "Keep it in there," I say. I get up and stare out of the kitchen window and catch a glimpse of sea between the houses. I remember Mum once saying that if we looked after *Moana*, she'd look after us. I can't help feeling that we've let her down.

"I'm coming with you, Dad," I say. "We can't just sell her to anybody. We owe her that, at least."

Dad nods. "I'll wait for you outside."

I get changed into my T-shirt and jeans and pull on my pale blue sweater. It's the only one without a hole. I walk with Dad across the town and up the steep hill to the row of new houses high along the clifftop.

The houses are hidden behind high walls and gated driveways. Big 4 x 4s and shiny cars sit outside the double garages. Dust blows our way from the building site for new houses on the other side of the road.

"Some people have all the luck," I say. "I bet *Moana* will be just a toy to them."

"Mr. Andersen sounds okay," says Dad.

"Is he the man who wants to buy her?"

Dad nods. "He says he's done a lot of sailing in the past. He owns a software company now in London. He says he's lived there fifteen years too long. That's why he wants to move down here. And he's got a son too, about your age."

"Great!" I mutter. I thought someone would buy *Moana* and take her away. But it will be worse, somehow, seeing someone else sailing her in the bay.

"This is the one," says Dad.

We stop outside a graveled drive at the end of the lane. Dad rings the bell on an intercom set into the wall, and the gates glide open automatically. A man stands in the doorway of the house in faded jeans and a T-shirt. I just stare at him. I had imagined Mr. Andersen in a suit and tie.

"Mr. Wood." He smiles, holding out his hand to Dad.

Dad shakes his. "Meet my daughter, Kara."

Mr. Andersen turns to me. "Pleased to meet you, Kara."

I dig my hands deep into my pockets and scrunch the gravel beneath my feet.

"Well, come on in," Mr. Andersen says. "I'll find my son. You'll have to meet him."

I stand with Dad in the hallway and watch Mr. Andersen walk away. The room is huge. The walls are white. The floor is sun-bleached wood. On a table beside the sweeping staircase sails a model tall-ship enveloped in a dome of glass. I press my nose against it and let my breath mist on the glass. I imagine pirates sailing through thick fog toward this ship. I want to watch my tiny pirates swing from the rigging. I want them to make the captain of this ship walk the plank into the painted sea.

"Great, isn't it?"

I look round. I hadn't heard Mr. Andersen return.

He looks through the misted glass too. "It's a replica of the *America*, the schooner that won the very first America's Cup around the Isle of Wight in 1851."

I straighten up and try to wipe the misted breath with my sleeve. I look around for his son, but he's not in the hallway.

"Come with me," he says, "I've found him at last. It'll be good for him to make some friends in this town."

Dad and I follow Mr. Andersen along the corridor and through a door into a bright and sun-filled room. Huge curved windows, floor to ceiling, fill one side. All I can see is sea, the vast expanse of the Atlantic. White leather sofas face the view.

"Kara, meet my son," says Mr. Andersen.

I turn around. A boy is sitting at a table, his back to the windows, staring at a big computer screen. I can only see the top of his head above the leather padding of his chair. He swivels around and frowns.

I scowl.

I can't believe it's him.

I fold my arms across my chest, and I know I can't hide the dislike on my face.

"We've already met before," I say.

11

It's Felix.

The new boy from school.

The boy who was rude to Daisy.

A ceiling fan whirs above us in the silence.

Mr. Andersen looks at Felix, eyebrows raised.

"We met at the school," says Felix. His voice is strangely nasal, as if he's got a bad cold, and his words are slurred.

Mr. Andersen's eyes flit between me and Felix.

He rubs his hand along the bottom of his chin. "Why don't you show Kara what you've been doing on the computer, Felix? I'll ask Mum to bring some lemonade. Would you like that, Kara?"

I nod and stare up at the whirling fan blades.

"Kara!" Dad gives me one of his sideways glares.

"Thank you, Mr. Andersen." I pronounce each word and glare back at Dad. "That would be very nice."

Mr. Andersen smiles briefly. "Good," he says. "Well, Jim, let's go and find somewhere quiet to talk about your lovely boat."

I watch them walk away. I feel cheated somehow, left behind. I want to stop Mr. Andersen from buying *Moana*. I turn back to Felix, but he's facing his computer again, his good hand tapping on the keys. I stand behind his chair and watch. The chair is large and padded with soft, white leather, like the sofas. Computer consoles are set into the armrests. I've seen gaming chairs like this in magazines and in the big gaming shops in Plymouth.

The only sound is the tapping of the computer keys and the whiring fan blades.

"Daisy was only trying to help, you know," I say. My voice sounds loud and echoes in the room.

Felix stops tapping on the keyboard. His fingers hover above the keys. "Well, I'm sorry if I offended her, but you can tell your sister I don't need her help."

"You can tell her you're sorry, yourself," I say. "Anyway, she's my cousin, not my sister."

"Whatever," says Felix. He starts tapping on the keys again. "Look, if other people get their kicks from laughing at me, it's their problem, not mine. It's no big deal."

A blank screen comes up on the computer. Felix hammers on the keys and slams his hand down on the desk. "But what *is* a big deal is *this*." He runs his hand through his hair. "There's no broadband here. How can you *live* like this?"

I dig my hands deep in my pockets. "What are you trying to do?"

Felix rolls his eyes. "Obvious, isn't it? I'm trying to log onto the Internet to play this game. But I can't connect. I'll have to play off-line."

A warrior in combat gear flashes on the screen. It revolves slowly around and around, surrounded by a choice of weapons. His clothes transform from military green to desert colors to polar white.

"At last," Felix says breathlessly. "Stealth Warriors," he says. "Have you played it before?"

I shake my head.

"Going up different levels gives you different levels of camouflage," he says. "I'm on level ten. At level ten, you can blend in with any background."

I rub my eyes. The computer screens at school always give me blinding headaches.

"What did you think of school?" I ask.

"Not much," he says. He doesn't take his eyes off the screen and taps the keyboard. His warrior appears against a city scene. "Look, watch this," he says. Six enemy warriors run down a road toward him. Felix presses something on his console, and his warrior starts to blend in with the background of bricks on the wall behind him. When the enemy arrive, all that remains is his shadow on the ground. "Cool, isn't it?"

I shrug my shoulders. But as I watch the screen, his warrior turns bright red. The biggest enemy warrior shoots him dead.

"Professor Lexus!" cries Felix. He flops back in his chair. "I should have known. My warrior turns red with anger when he sees him. I'll have to start again now."

I don't want to watch Felix play his computer game. I can't stop thinking about what Dad and Mr. Andersen are talking about right now. Does he want to buy our boat? I walk over to the windows and look out at the sea. The sun pours in, and despite the fans, it's hot in here. I pull my sweater off and leave it on the floor. A fulmar glides past, angling its outstretched, stubby wings to ride the wind. The sea glitters in the sunlight. It looks calm, but the base of Gull Rock is white with plumes of spray. A sailing boat is leaning in the wind. It dips up and down through waves. It's rougher than it looks out there today.

Footsteps tap on the floor. I turn to see a woman walking over with a tray of drinks. I recognize her from the café. It's Mrs. Andersen, the woman Felix was arguing with.

"You must be Kara," she says.

I nod.

"Felix isn't letting you play, I see," she says.

Either Felix hasn't heard or is ignoring her.

Mrs. Andersen smiles but says loud enough for him to hear, "He always has to be in the control seat."

"I'm not that interested in computer games, anyway," I say.

"Good for you," she says. "Hear that, Felix? You could take a break from it."

Felix gets up from his chair and walks over to us. His steps are short and jerky. I notice his bare toes hit the floor before his heels. He picks up a glass of lemonade in his good hand and glares at his mother. "If we were back in London, I'd be out somewhere with my mates." He glugs back his drink and crams a cookie from the tray into his mouth. I guess this was what they were arguing about in the café yesterday.

I pick up my drink and look back out the window.

"Amazing, isn't it?" says Mrs. Andersen. "We bought this place for the view."

I sip my drink. It's fresh lemonade from real lemons, not the fizzy bottled stuff.

"We saw dolphins two nights ago," says Mrs. Andersen, "right from this very window."

I look across the wide sweep of the bay. "I saw them too."

Mrs. Andersen smiles. "They're such clever animals. We saw them at a water park in Florida. Do you remember, Felix? All those tricks they did?"

"Amazing," says Felix. He doesn't try to hide the

sarcasm in his voice. "Just how exciting can it get, watching yet another dolphin jump through a hoop?"

I wonder how he thinks the dolphins must feel, jumping hoop after hoop every day in a small pool, but I don't trust myself to speak. Instead I stare into my drink. All I want to do is find Dad and leave, but I don't even know where he is right now.

Mrs. Andersen ignores Felix and turns to me. "So, have you and your dad always lived here?"

I nod. I wish she'd stop trying to be so friendly. "Dad's a fisherman," I say. Even as I say it, I think how stupid that sounds. How will he catch fish without his boat?

"And your mum?" says Mrs. Andersen. "What does she do?"

I swallow hard. It feels as though the ground has dropped away from me. I tighten my hands around my glass and stumble on my words. "Away," I say, "Mum's away right now. She's . . ." But my voice trails off. I don't know what to say.

Mrs. Andersen swirls the ice in her lemonade round and round. It clinks against the glass. She looks as relieved as I feel when we hear Dad's voice and see him and Mr. Andersen come through the doorway.

Mr. Andersen smiles. "Well, Kara, you've got a very clever dad. The *Moana*'s a wonderful boat. There's real craftsmanship there."

I want to say something to stop him from buying *Moana*, but I lose my moment, because I've never heard anyone talk about Dad like that before.

Mrs. Andersen leans her head to one side. "Well, Matt?"

Mr. Andersen grins and looks at Dad. "Can I tell them, Jim?"

I look at Dad, but can't read his face. Surely he hasn't agreed to sell *Moana*.

Felix is frowning too.

Mr. Andersen smiles. "Jim, here, has offered to take us out tomorrow for a trial run on *Moana*."

Felix finishes his drink and puts his glass down on the table. "I'm busy."

"Not all day," says Mr. Andersen.

I notice him frown at Felix.

"What's the weather going to be like?" asks Mrs. Andersen.

Dad looks out to sea. The waves are capped with white horses, and I see the top-most branches of a tree in the next garden sway in the wind.

"It'll be a bit lively out there today," says Dad. "But the wind's meant to die down tomorrow, so we should be okay."

Mrs. Andersen glances at Felix and then her husband. "I think it's best if you just go, Matt. Felix doesn't want to, anyway."

Mr. Andersen shoves his hands deep into his pockets. "Fine," he says. "Fine." Another frown creases on his face. But I can't help smiling deep inside. He's the only one of them interested in *Moana*. Maybe he won't buy her after all.

Mr. Andersen leads Dad and me back into the

hall. He opens the door and the cool outside air rushes through.

"Wait a sec," I say. "I've left my sweater." I turn and run back to the room. I hope I can slip in without Felix noticing, but he's standing by the windows, looking out to sea. I cross the room to fetch my sweater. He doesn't even turn to look at me.

"What's out there?" he asks.

I look beyond him to the wide, blue sea.

"There's nothing there," he says. "Nothing until you get to America, and that's where I'm going one day."

I tie my sweater round my waist and start walking to the door.

"No offense," says Felix, "but it's a dump round here. There's nothing to do."

I stop and turn. "So go back to London," I say.

Felix rolls his eyes. "According to Dad, I need some good sea air, and according to Mum, London's becoming far too dangerous."

"It can't be that bad."

"Of course it isn't," says Felix. "And I actually have a life back there."

"So, make them go back," I say.

Felix presses his head against the glass and stares through his reflection out to the sea. "Believe me, I intend to."

I spin on my heels and walk toward the door. I feel a surge of hope inside, because maybe Mr. Andersen won't buy *Moana* if Felix can make them all go back to London.

I stop by the door and turn. "You're right not to go sailing tomorrow. It's far too rough. It can get pretty wild out there."

Felix snorts a laugh. "It doesn't bother me," he says. "I just can't see the point of going up and down in a stupid boat." He walks away in his short, jerky steps to sit in his control chair and starts tapping at the keyboard.

I smile because he hasn't fooled me. "It's no game out there," I say. "When the wind is screaming in your face and the waves are coming over the sides, there are no second chances. You can't just die and start again."

Felix's fingers hammer the keys, but I know he's listening.

"Just how brave are you," I say, "when the real world is out of your control?"

Felix's fingers stop tapping.

I shut the door and smile, leaving Felix and deep silence in the room.

12

"I've put a thermos of coffee on the side to take," says Aunt Bev, "and some saffron buns. Let's hope it makes Mr. Andersen want to buy *Moana.*"

Dad's fishing tackle, spare life jacket, and a bucket of bait are piled by the kitchen door. I squash the thermos inside the canvas bag with the rest of the picnic, and place the yellow buns on top. Dad's already packed some pasties, crisps, and a large bottle of lemonade and plastic cups.

"He'll be expecting sushi, not pasties," I say.

Dad looks up. "What's that?"

"Nothing." I slide down against the door frame and push my foot against the corner of the bag. I hear the crack of the plastic cups and feel my foot press against the soft bag of pasties. I want the meat and onions to split through the bag and stick against the thermos and the crisps. I pick a currant from one of the buns and roll it between my fingers.

"Leave that." Aunt Bev glares at me from over her magazine. "Mr. Andersen won't want half-eaten buns."

Daisy is cutting pictures out from magazines and catalogs and sticking them on paper. She stops cutting, scissors in midair, and frowns. "His son's the one from the café, isn't he?"

I nod. "He's the new boy in our school."

Daisy's frown deepens. "There's something wrong with him, isn't there?"

"You're right there," I say. "He's rude, and I don't like him."

Dad turns the cold tap and watches water swirl into an old plastic bottle. "Mr. Andersen told me Felix has cerebral palsy," he says.

Aunt Bev looks up and sucks air sharply through her teeth. "I've just been reading about that in my *Pregnancy* magazine. It happens if a baby doesn't get enough oxygen to the brain before it's born." She covers her belly with her hand and holds up one magazine. "There's a story in here about a girl with it. She can't walk or talk. Stuck in a wheelchair, she is, for life."

"That boy's not in a wheelchair," says Daisy.

Dad turns off the tap and caps the bottle. "I think it affects some worse than others."

Aunt Bev closes the magazine and shakes her head. "I pity his poor parents."

"Me too," I say. It's the first time Aunt Bev and I have agreed on something. "I don't know how they can stand him."

"Kara!" Aunt Bev frowns at me. "You shouldn't say that. He's . . ." She pauses, as if she can't find the words she's looking for. "You should feel sorry for him, is all I'm saying. He's not like you or me."

I pick up the picnic bag and walk out of the door. "Doesn't seem to stop him from being rude," I say.

Dad's standing inside *Moana*, pulling the mainsail up the mast. "We'll have to put a reef in," he says. "It's a bit fresh out there."

I look out through the gap in the harbor walls. The sea beyond is lumpy and flecked with white. "It's not that bad," I say. "We've been out in worse with full sails."

Dad runs a fold along the bottom of the sail to make the mainsail smaller. "We're not racing," he says. "We're giving Mr. Andersen a gentle trip out."

"We should charge him for it," I say. "He's got enough money."

I heave the picnic bag and swimming bag and spare towels into the boat and push them into the locker under the foredeck. I tie the bucket with the bait around the mast base to keep it from rolling across the deck as we sail. I want it to be just me today. Just me and Dad. I don't want anyone else on our boat.

"Here's Mr. Andersen," says Dad.

I look up to see Mr. Andersen walking along the dock followed by Mrs. Andersen and Felix. I'm surprised they've come along to see him off. The wooden boards of the dock bounce with their footsteps, and I see Felix stumble to his knees. His mother tries to help him up, but he brushes her away.

"All set?" asks Mr. Andersen. He puts his bag beside the boat.

Dad nods. "It should be fun out there today."

Mr. Andersen glances back at Felix. "I hope it's still okay with you, but Felix has changed his mind. He'd like to come along too. I've borrowed a life jacket for him."

"That's fine with me," says Dad.

Felix glares at me and looks away.

I climb out onto the dock to take Mr. Andersen's bag.

Mrs. Andersen's scarf flaps across her face, and she pulls it free. "I really don't think this is a great idea, Matt," she says. "It's too windy today."

"It's fine," says Mr. Andersen. "What d'you think, Jim?"

Dad looks up at the flag on the chandlery. It's flying full out, rippling in the wind. The top branches in the tree beyond are swaying. "It's a force five, I reckon," he says. "But I checked the weather report, and it's going to settle down later."

I dig my hands into my pockets and take a sly glance at Felix. "Looks like a force six or seven to me," I say.

Mrs. Andersen wraps her coat around her and folds her arms. "I don't think you should go, Felix."

Mr. Andersen turns to her. "But, Sarah . . ."

She lowers her head next to his, but I can still hear them. The wind is blowing this way.

"Anything could happen out there," she says. "What if you capsize, what then?"

Mr. Andersen runs his hands through his hair. "Nothing's going to happen, Sarah."

"Look, Matt, buy the damn boat if you must," she snaps. I glance at Dad, and I know he can hear them too. "But don't expect either of us to step foot in it."

"I want to go, Mum." Felix is grim faced, staring at the water. "I'll be fine."

I pull my life jacket on, zip it up, and pull the Velcro cords tight. I can't imagine Felix enjoying this trip.

Mrs. Andersen glares at Felix. "What's changed your mind?"

Felix doesn't take his eyes off the water. "I want to go."

Mrs. Andersen spins around to her husband. "Have you got your mobile on you at least?"

"Yes, Sarah," he says. He puts his arms out to hug her, but she walks away. The thud of her footsteps on the wooden boards jars through the bare soles of my feet.

I watch Mr. Andersen fasten Felix's life jacket and help him into the boat. Felix struggles to swing his left leg over. One leg is stiff and locked straight out, and his arm is bent and curled. *Moana* sways underneath him, and his dad catches him as he tumbles forward.

"You might find it easier to sit up at the front," says Dad. "There's more space and there's a handhold."

Felix pulls himself up on the seat and grips the brass handle with his good hand. His knuckles turn white, and I feel a twinge of guilt run through me. I hadn't actually thought how hard this could be for him.

I untie the mooring rope and push *Moana* away from the dock. Dad sets her sails, and we slide out between the harbor walls.

The first wave hits us side on, and I see Felix lurch sideways. He stares down at the floor and presses himself against the side, bracing himself for the next wave. He doesn't look up until we are far out in the bay. It's less choppy, but an ocean swell rolls in from the Atlantic in gray-green hills of waves. Mr. Andersen is leaning back, smiling, the sun shining on his face. He holds the jib sheet in his hand, keen to help Dad sail *Moana*. But Felix is looking at his feet again.

And he's a sickly shade of green.

I slide over beside him. "It helps if you look out of the boat," I say.

Felix looks up briefly and scowls at me. "I'm not interested in the view."

I lean back and stare out to sea. "What I mean is, if you fix your eyes on the horizon, you won't feel so sick."

Felix nods and looks out beyond the boat.

"We'll check our lobster traps, if that's okay by you, Mr. Andersen!" shouts Dad. "Then we'll go on to Gull Rock where we can stop for lunch."

"That's fine by us!" Mr. Andersen shouts back.

He lets the jib out a little as Dad turns away from the wind. "How many traps do you and your dad have, Kara?"

"About twenty."

"Do you catch much?"

"Enough," I say. I turn my back on him, fold my arms on *Moana*'s side, and look out to sea. I want to see the dolphins again. I want to see them leaping through our bow waves. *Moana*'s wake runs in lace ribbons out behind us. The sunlight sparkles in the sea, like stars. Soon we won't have this. We won't have any of this anymore.

We round the headland and pass along the rugged coastline of rocky inlets and deep shelving coves. Bright orange buoys of crab and lobster traps bob on the water, marking the lobster traps beneath. A man in his boat waves to us. I see the initials *TL* on his buoys. It's Ted from the *Merry Mermaid* checking his traps. I remember painting Dad's initials on our buoys. I painted flowers on them, too, big white ones. Dad said he never heard the last of it down at the pub. They called him the flower pot man for months. They teased him too, because Mum made him use traditional withy traps made from willow, not the modern metal and mesh nylon ones.

Dad spills some wind from the sails, and we slow down toward the mouth of the rocky inlet where we keep our lobster traps. Two ravens croak from the clifftop. Waves slap against the rocks, and gulls wheel and scream in a tight circle above the cove. I crane my neck to look, because there must be something there to pull the gulls and ravens in. A buoy with painted flowers bobs loose on the water, like a small child's lost balloon. It trails a blue rope in a long line out behind it.

Suddenly I feel sick deep inside, because something here feels so wrong.

A roar of engines cuts through the air, and a puff of black smoke drifts up into the sky. An orange ribbed inflatable boat bursts from our cove. It rears over a wave and smacks down into the water, sending up spumes of flying spray.

It passes close and slews in a tight arc around us. *Moana* rocks in its wake, and I have to put my arm out not to fall. I see Dougie Evans at the wheel, a grim smile on his face. Jake holds up his hand, his finger and thumb out in a loser sign.

But my heart is thumping in my chest because Jake's words repeat over and over again in my head.

"Soon, you and your dad will have nothing left."

13

The small inlet is empty of our buoys, almost.

Two more orange buoys float against the rocks, trailing cut ropes across the water. I see our initials on them, and the flowers. There's one buoy floating in the water near us. Dad hauls it in and pulls up the rope. But I can see it's coming up too quickly. Dad pulls on the rope, hand over hand, not coiling it but spilling it in a tangled mess inside the boat. The lobster trap comes up over the side, a wreck of smashed-up wicker. The door has been wrenched off, and the curved funnel of the trap has been cut apart. It's useless now.

Dad just stares at the mangled mess in his hands. "That's all of them gone, Kara," he says.

I stare out to the orange rib inflatable disappearing into the distance, spumes of white spray flying in its wake.

Mr. Andersen is sitting forward, his face a tight frown. "What happened here?"

"Let's call the police, Dad," I say.

Dad shakes his head. "No point. There's no proof is there? It's his word against mine."

"But, Dad . . ."

Dad shoves the remains of the trap on the seat next to me. He forces a smile to his face and turns to Mr. Andersen. "Let's go for lunch, shall we?"

He pushes the tiller over hard, the boom swings out and the sail snaps tight.

Moana lurches forward.

I sit back and watch the cove recede into the jumble of boulders along the coastline. An empty Coke can bobs in a slick of engine oil. I hate Jake Evans. I hate him for everything he is. My eyes burn hot with tears, and this time I can't stop them falling.

I glance at Dad, but his eyes are focused out to sea, a deep frown line on his face. He's sailing *Moana* roughly through the water. She jars against the waves, each one slamming into us as we roll and pitch.

Felix is staring at his feet, his face a deeper shade of green. Each wave thumps the boat against his back. I try and warn Dad, but it's too late. Felix lurches forward, vomits, and whacks his head against the deck.

"Felix!" yells Mr. Andersen.

Dad turns *Moana* into the wind and lets her sails flap loose.

"Take the tiller, Kara," orders Dad. "Keep up into the wind."

I sit at the stern and watch Mr. Andersen wipe Felix's face with a towel. Dad empties the bait bucket, fills it with seawater, and helps clean up Felix too. Felix is a deathly shade of white. His whole body shakes, and he looks like he'll be sick again. Mr. Andersen props him up and pulls a water bottle from his bag. Dad fetches the first aid kit from the locker and kneels down to clean a cut on Felix's face.

"I think we should head back," says Dad.

Mr. Andersen rinses the towel in the sea and wrings it out. "You're right." He hangs the towel across the seat beside him. "Sorry, Felix, Mum was right on this one. I shouldn't have let you come today."

Felix leans back against the seat and glares at me. "I'm fine," he says. "Let's go on."

Mr. Andersen crouches next to him. "You don't look great. I think it's best if we go back."

Felix takes a swig of water from his bottle. "I said I'm fine."

Mr. Andersen looks at Dad and shrugs his shoulders.

"If you're sure," says Dad. "We can stop off at Gull Rock and head back after that."

Felix nods and fixes his eyes out to sea.

I watch a dark patch of wind-ruffled water sweep toward us. *Moana*'s sails flap in the passing gust.

"The wind's not so strong now," says Dad. "We'll let *Moana* have full sails."

I lean forward, in line with Felix, as Dad and Mr. Andersen take the reefs out of the sails. "You don't have to go on, you know. You've proved your point."

Felix takes another swig from the water bottle and doesn't even look at me.

Dad slides around to the back of *Moana* and gives me a gentle shove. "Go up to the front, Kara. I thought Felix could have a go at sailing. Would you like that, Felix? It'll take your mind off seasickness if you can concentrate on something else."

Felix nods. He looks slightly better, a paler shade of green now.

I sit up at the front of the boat with Mr. Andersen,

but can't help looking back at Dad and Felix. A pang of jealousy runs through me, and I try to push it away. Dad taught me to sail like this, sitting with him by the tiller, allowing me to test the wind and feel it in the sails. Felix can't control the mainsail and the tiller with only one good arm. It takes two hands for that. But I watch Dad show him how to adjust the mainsail, when to pull it in and how to spill air if we heel over too far.

Moana slices through the water on a course set for Gull Rock. We're running fast and smooth. Mr. Andersen and I have to lean right out to balance her. I run my hands in the bow waves that furl along *Moana*'s sides. Her sails above us are curved and taut like birds' wings. We're racing through the water. It feels as if we're flying almost.

I look back again to see Dad and Felix, big grins stuck on both their faces. That pang of jealousy hasn't gone away. It's not because of Dad, this time. It's because of Felix. For someone who's never sailed before, he's good at sailing.

He's far too good.

I don't want to admit it, but Felix Andersen is a born natural.

Dad takes over near Gull Rock and guides *Moana* into the crescent-shaped cove that faces the mainland shore. It's sheltered here. The waves that heave against the seaward cliffs of Gull Rock swirl round here in foam-topped eddies. Mr. Andersen drops the anchor, and Dad lets down the sails.

Felix's eyes are shining and the color is back in his face. "That was *so* cool."

Dad sits back and grins. "That was some sailing, Felix. Don't you think so, Kara?"

I shrug my shoulders. "It was okay."

Mr. Andersen can't take the smile off his face. He punches Felix on the shoulder. "I told you you'd like it."

Dad pulls the picnic bag out from the locker. "You could enter the regatta race with sailing like that."

Felix just sits there with a massive grin.

"What race is that?" asks Mr. Andersen.

"It's the one held every summer on the last day of August," says Dad. "Any sailing boat can enter. It's a race from the harbor around Gull Rock and back."

I pull my knees up to my chest. I don't want Dad to be telling them any of this. It's *our* boat, *our* race. I look out at the shelving pebble bay and the sheer cliffs of Gull Rock and feel an ache deep in my chest. This is our special place. It could be the last time we ever come out here.

"Pasty, anyone?" asks Dad.

The smell of cooked meat and onions drifts across the boat.

He holds one of the squashed pasties out to Felix. "Are you up to this?"

Felix nods. "I'm starving."

Dad pours out lemonade into plastic cups, balancing them on the wooden seats.

Mr. Andersen takes a mouthful of pasty and

leans back with his feet up on the seats. He pulls his hat over his eyes and smiles. "I have to say, this has to be the best meal I've had in years."

I don't touch my pasty. I can't imagine watching someone else sail *Moana* in the regatta race. I want to forget about Felix and his dad. I want to forget about Jake Evans, too. All I want is to escape.

"Can I have a quick swim, Dad?" I ask.

Dad nods, and I reach into the locker for my mask and snorkel. I peel my shorts and T-shirt off to my swimming costume, underneath.

Mr. Andersen looks at Felix. "Why don't you go too? You could clean yourself off a bit."

Felix's shorts are patterned with crusted sea salt and flecks of dried vomit. He looks down at them and shrugs his shoulders. "Okay."

I stare down at my feet. I want to swim by myself, not have Felix tagging along.

"Is that okay, Kara?" asks Mr. Andersen.

"There can be strong currents out there," I say.

"You're only swimming to the rocks," says Dad.

"Felix is a good swimmer," says Mr. Andersen.

"And it's cold too," I say.

Dad finds a spare face-mask. "Here, Felix. You should see a lot today, the water's crystal clear."

I curl my toes over *Moana*'s side and look down. My reflection is rippled like the water. When I was small, I used to think it was a magic mirror, a secret entrance to another world below.

I take a deep breath of air.

And dive.

Cold water rushes through my hair and across my skin. I twist and look up to the surface, a dolphin's-eye view of *Moana*'s shadowed hull. Shafts of sunlight filter through the water, reaching into deep, deep blue. I swim toward the rocks that lie submerged beneath the cliffs. Purple jewel anemones line the narrow crevices. Small silver sand eels flit between the rippling strands of seaweed. I spread my arms and soar above this world, above a landscape of mountains, valleys, and vast grasslands of green kelp.

When I come up for air, Felix is right behind me. I didn't think he'd be able to swim so fast. I hadn't really thought he could swim at all. I push my hair from my eyes and tread water beside him.

Felix lifts the corner of his face-mask to drain some water that's leaked inside. "Can't see a thing," he says.

His mask is steamed up and blurry. "Spit in it," I say.

Felix frowns at me. "What?"

"Spit in it. It stops the mask from steaming up."

Felix pulls his mask off and spits inside, rubbing the saliva with this thumb. He struggles to pull the strap over his head again. I almost help him, but see Dad and Mr. Andersen watching, so I swim away, toward a submerged shelf of rock lined with fine white sand.

Felix joins me and we drift side by side, arms outstretched, our fingertips almost touching. I stare down, hypnotized. Nothing is still. The sea floor is a changing pattern of swaying seaweed and shifting

sand. A silver river of tiny fish thread through the kelp, each fish no longer than my thumb. But there is something else moving through the water too, a creature I've heard about but never seen before.

It's here now, right now.

I catch a fleeting glimpse of zebra stripe between the kelp, and then it's gone.

I nudge Felix in the side and point.

He bursts up to the surface, and I take a gasp of breath too.

I shake the water from my hair. "Did you see it?" I ask.

Felix pushes his mask up from his face. "See what?"

"Down there in the kelp, you must've seen it."

"What, Kara?"

"Stealth Killers," I say and can't help grinning. "Level ten."

14

I float beside him, looking down. I see it again, this time a flash of dark against the pale sand, but it's changing all the time.

Felix bursts up again from the water, and I lift my head up too.

"I still can't see anything down there," he says.

I sweep my wet hair from my face and look at Felix. "That's because you aren't looking right," I say. "I'll point. Just keep looking at the sand."

I dive under to skim the pale sand floor. Scraps of seaweed and a crab-shell case rock back and forth. I can't see the animal I'm looking for at first. Its camouflage is far too good. But then I see it watching me from the sand below me. Only the horseshoe-shaped black pupils of its eyes give it away. The speckled pattern of its body perfectly matches the sand beneath. I reach out to touch it, but it rises upward, away from me, and stops midwater, changing color in an instant to bright red. It looks like a small, deflated beach ball with long tentacles at one end. Its body is fringed by a rim of fins that ripple along each side. The tentacles stick straight out in front of it, like a sword.

I burst upward to catch a breath of air.

Felix takes a breath too. "What *is* that?"

"Cuttlefish," I say.

Felix frowns. "What old ladies feed to parrots?"

I roll my eyes. "That's the cuttlebone, its skeleton inside."

"I want another look," says Felix.

We float on the surface, faces down, slowly spinning with the current. We are skydivers looking at a world far, far below.

The red cuttlefish is still there, watching us watching it. It's a strange feeling, being observed like this. Another cuttlefish swims into view, a pale brown one with a perfect white square patch on its back. I remember Mum telling me that males and females come to breed and lay their eggs on kelp in the spring and summer. The red cuttlefish is changing color again. Its head and tentacles are still bright red, but its body now has zebra stripes of black and white. The stripes begin to ripple across its body in moving patterns. The brown cuttlefish is changing too. Bands of dark color sweep across its body.

I see Felix beside me take a breath and dive down. He reaches out his hand. His fingers almost touch the tentacles of the red cuttlefish, but both cuttlefish propel backward, and he is left groping in a billowing black cloud of ink. Felix bursts upward again for air. I keep looking underwater, but when the ink clears, both cuttlefish have disappeared. They could be anywhere by now, perfectly camouflaged against the pale sand or dark gray rock.

Mr. Andersen helps to haul us out of the water. He wraps Felix in a big beach towel, and Dad wraps my blanket round me too.

"What did you two see over there?" asks Mr. Andersen. "You were there for ages."

"Cuttlefish," I say.

Mr. Andersen turns to Felix, "Cuttlefish?"

Felix nods. He can't stop his teeth from chattering. "They were amazing, Dad. You've got to go and look. Just don't try and touch one, like I did."

"I think we should take a look," says Dad. "I've not seen them before myself."

Dad and Mr. Andersen strip off their T-shirts and jump into the water with the face-masks and snorkels.

I sink down out of the wind and take a bite of pasty.

Felix takes a bite from his pasty too, and stares out to sea, his face lit up in golden light.

"I've not seen anything like that before," he says.

I look at him and nod. "It's not just there," I say. "It goes on and on. There's a whole coral reef down there, and I'm going to see all that someday." I finish my pasty and shake the crumbs from my blanket. "Mum said when I'm sixteen I can learn to scuba dive. She said she'd take me out to see the reef. If it's still there, that is."

Felix slides down beside me and leans against *Moana*'s curved hull. "Why wouldn't it be?"

"The dredging ban is lifted in a week's time," I say. "Then, dredgers from up and down the coast will come and haul their metal rakes across the seabed for scallops. It's not just scallops they'll be ripping out, but everything else, all those things you've seen today. There'll be nothing left."

Felix stuffs the end crust of his pasty in his mouth and sucks his fingers. "So stop them," he says.

I glare at him. "Easy for you to say. What can *I* do? Just sit out here in a rubber dinghy and turn their trawlers away?"

Felix rubs his towel in his hair. "I don't know," he says. "But if it meant that much to me, I wouldn't give up without a fight."

I pull broken pieces of wicker from the tattered lobster trap and look at Felix. "You don't know Dougie Evans. No one can stop him. No one."

"Who's he?"

"The man you saw who wrecked our lobster traps," I say. "That's him."

"So why's he got it in for you?"

I flick the pieces out into the water. I don't know how much Felix knows about me and Dad. "Mum got the dredging ban put in place for a ten-year study of the reef," I say. I sit up on one of the seats and stare out to sea. "But she never got to finish her research. Time ran out. And her funding ran out too. That's why the ban is being lifted. She never got to show her final results."

"So Dougie Evans wasn't happy about the ban?" says Felix.

I nod. "He said Mum was a greenie foreigner

who couldn't tell him what to do. But all the local fishermen were on her side, especially when she found out Dougie Evans was trying to sell his fish as line-caught fish."

"What difference does that make?" asks Felix.

"Line-caught fish is more expensive, but people will pay more because it's dolphin friendly. Hundreds of dolphins drown in fishing nets each year."

"So he hates you because your mum found out he was a cheat?" asks Felix.

"It wasn't just that," I say. "Dougie had another son, too. Aaron. He was seventeen when he was swept off one of Dougie's trawlers in a bad storm. Dougie blamed Mum, saying that if he'd been able to fish closer to the shore where the reef is, his son would be alive today."

Felix gives a small laugh. "And my mum thought London was dangerous! She thought we'd moved to a safe, sleepy fishing town. I think she's in for a shock."

15

Dad lets Felix take the tiller as a light breeze takes us home. The golden sunlight of afternoon slants across the bay. I stare down into the water hoping to see the white dolphin. Once or twice I almost imagine something white rushing beneath our bow waves, twisting in our wake. I want it to be her. I want to see her, because maybe then it means we'll keep *Moana*. But instead all I see are cloud reflections skimming across the water.

Mrs. Andersen is waiting for us on the harbor wall, twisting her scarf around her hands. She waves as we slide through the gap into the deep water moorings. Mr. Andersen waves back and Felix grins and gives the thumbs-up. His face has caught the sun and his hair is salt-crusted and windswept. He looks like a different boy from the one we took out this morning.

The tide is too low to take *Moana* to her mooring site at the dock, so Dad takes her alongside the trawlers and the lifeboat.

"We'll help you take down the sails and sort her out," says Mr. Andersen.

Dad smiles. "We'll be just fine. You go on home. Kara and I will wait for the tide to come in and take her to her mooring."

Mr. Andersen puts out his hand and pumps Dad's hand up and down. "Well, thanks, Jim. It's been great. I'll be in touch."

Felix stands up and steadies himself on *Moana*'s side. His dad helps him out onto the rough steps cut into the harbor wall. Felix opens his mouth as if he's about to say something but then turns, grasps the rusty handrail, and lifts one foot to the next step. I watch Mr. Andersen sling his bag over his shoulder and climb up behind Felix, up to the top, to Mrs. Andersen peering anxiously down.

I tidy up *Moana* and wipe the salt spray from her decks. Dad helps me stuff the wrecked lobster trap in a spare canvas bag.

He slings it on the floor and sighs. "It's not as if we're going to be using them much longer."

I wipe up crumbs from the seats and tip them out into the harbor water. I look down to see small fish dart up and take the crumbs. "D'you think Mr. Andersen will buy her?"

"We'll have to see," Dad says. "He's going to have a chat with his wife and ring me later."

We have to wait another hour for the tide to creep in. I hear it sucking across the mud, filling in the lugworm holes. Two oystercatchers run up and down the shoreline, stopping to probe their orange bills deep into the mud. I help paddle *Moana* across to her mooring, watching the oar swirl through the still water.

"It was a good trip today," I say. "*Moana* sailed well."

Dad smiles. "She never lets us down, does she?"

I shake my head, but can't help feeling that's exactly what we're doing to her.

We walk back to Aunt Bev's through the town in early evening, tired and sunburned. I flop down on the sofa. Daisy's watching a game show on TV, and Aunt Bev is knitting booties for the baby. I hardly move until the phone rings. I strain my ears to hear who Dad is talking to.

I hear Dad say good-bye and put the phone back. I don't want to know. I don't want to hear what he's got to say. Aunt Bev puts her knitting down and glances at the door.

Dad walks in, sits down next to me, and runs his hands through his hair.

Aunt Bev mutes the volume. "Well?" she asks.

Dad shakes his head and frowns. "Mr. Andersen doesn't want to buy her."

I sit up. "What?"

Aunt Bev glares at him. "I said you should've dropped the price."

"It's not that," says Dad. "Mr. Andersen seemed keen at the time, but he said something about listening to Felix, and 'doing the right thing.'"

"They're going back to London," I say. "That's what they're going to do."

Aunt Bev snatches up her knitting. "Let's hope you find another buyer soon, Jim. It's the only way you'll pay those debts." She shakes her head and turns the volume back up.

But I can't take the grin off my face.

Maybe it *was* the white dolphin I saw beneath the bow waves. Mr. Andersen has changed his mind. He doesn't want to buy *Moana*.

Moana's still our boat.

She's ours for now at least.

16

I sit in Mrs. Carter's office after school while she watches me press tape across the last of the ripped pages of the Bible. Some of the pages were never found. Lost at sea. Presumed drowned.

I close the Bible and push it across the table. "I'm sorry," I mutter.

School finished half an hour ago. Through the office window, I can see some of my class in the playground beyond the school gates. Jake is sitting next to Ethan, twirling round and round on the preschool swings.

Mrs. Carter leans forward, elbows on the table. "Kara, did you know that I asked your father to come and see me today?"

I nod. Dad said she wanted to see him about me breaking Jake Evans's nose.

"And you know that while I have every sympathy for your situation, I cannot accept violence in the school?"

I nod again.

"I've told your father that if this happens again, we will have no choice but to suspend you from school."

Part of me wants to laugh. It hardly seems a punishment. I'd do anything not to have to come to school.

Mrs. Carter opens the Bible at one of the ripped pages. Her voice is suddenly soft and measured. "Your father and I spoke about this, too."

I frown and look down at the Bible. I've already said that I was sorry. I don't like to think about them talking about me, discussing me behind my back.

Mrs. Carter pulls her chair closer to the table. "Can I tell you a story, Kara?"

All I want to do is go.

"It's about a man," she says, "who dreams he is walking with God along a beach.'

I stare at my hands. I'm in no mood for one of Mrs. Carter's Bible stories.

"The man looks back at the path they have taken and he sees that in one place there is only one set of footprints. He's angry at God and says, 'You left me when I most needed you. See, there is only one set of footprints in the sand.'"

I pick at a loose corner of tape holding the page together. A memory of Mum flashes through me: the time she carried me out of the sea after I'd stepped on a weaver fish. I'd wrapped my arms around her neck, pain throbbing through my foot. I'd clung to her and watched her bare footprints trail out behind us. I look up at Mrs. Carter. I already know the ending to her story.

She smiles at me. "God said to the man, 'I never left you. Those footsteps you see are mine. They are when I carried you.'"

I close the Bible and slide it over to Mrs. Carter.

"God never leaves us, Kara."

"What if you don't believe in God?" I ask. The words have tumbled out before I could stop them. I know Mum doesn't believe in Him.

I think Mrs. Carter is going to give one of her assembly speeches, but she doesn't. She gets up from her seat and puts the Bible back on the shelf next to the atlas and the dictionary. She sits back down on the table edge. "You know, Kara," she says. "When you love someone, they never really leave you, ever. Some part of them always stays with you deep down inside."

I nod and shift in my seat. I feel hot and stuffy all at once. I don't want her talking to me about all this. I just want to go.

"You can go home now." Mrs. Carter is smiling at me. "It was good to talk today, Kara."

I almost run out of her office and then grab my coat from my locker. I don't want to go out through the front gates and everyone in the park. I feel too churned up inside. Instead of heading out of the main doors, I walk along the corridor to the staff parking lot on the other side of school. If I take the top road out of town, I can swing back along the coastal footpath without anyone, especially Jake and Ethan, seeing me.

It's not just that. I want to give myself an excuse to go back to the cove, to look for the dolphins again. Dad's not expecting me home for at least another hour, so I still have time to spare. Maybe I'll have time to go and see *Moana*. I can't believe she's ours still. Felix wasn't at school today, so I guess I'm right and he's going back to London after all. I'm glad he's not buying *Moana*, but part of me wanted to see him at school today, because when he saw the cuttlefish and the reef, it seemed to mean something to him, too.

The road from the school winds up the hill under

a tunnel of branches throwing zebra stripes of deep shadow on the pavement. Beyond the tunnel of trees, I catch glimpses of the sea in gaps and gateways between the high banks of the hedgerows. Goosegrass and bindweed scramble over stunted wind-bent hazel. I climb the steps to the wheat fields and run along the stubbly footpath to the cliffs. Above, the sky is clear and blue. A breeze carries the coconut smell of gorse from the bushes along the clifftop, and a single seagull hangs in midair, angling its wings to catch the updraft from the sea.

I scramble through the gorse and look down. The water in the cove below glitters in the sunlight. I have to shade my eyes against the flashes of reflected glare. But I see something else moving through the water. The blue-gray body of a dolphin twists and turns in the shallows. I can hear it calling, its high-pitched whistles. It surges forward in a spray of surf, trying to beach itself on the sand. I can't believe it's really here, as if it's me it's waiting for.

I scramble down the cliff and jump the last few feet to the small beach uncovered by the ebbing tide. I run through the maze of boulders. My feet slap on the soft, wet sand. Pooled water and pale boulders reflect bright white light. I don't stop. A flock of seagulls lifts into the air and a raven croaks and hops down from a boulder in the shallow waves. Another raven flaps up from the pale boulder and flies away. Its wing tips almost brush my head.

And that's when I see it.

Even though the boulder is snagged with seaweed, it's too smooth and white to be a rock here. It's not a rock at all.

It's a dolphin.

It's the white dolphin lying beached upon the shore. Small waves run in and furl around her. But the sand is wet and hard. The tide mark of scum and seaweed curls around her tail flukes. The tide has turned and is ebbing out to sea.

The other dolphin in the water rushes at the shore again. I was stupid to think it was me she was waiting for. She's not waiting for me at all. She's trying to reach her calf beside me on the sand.

I've never seen a dolphin so close up before. I've seen them in the distance and in books, but I've never been right next to one. I guess the white dolphin must be young, but I can tell she's not newborn. She's maybe one of last year's calves. I follow the curve of her back and dorsal fin to her tail flukes. She's not really white at all. Her body is pale pink, and her fins and tail are tinged with blue. Deep scratches, dark with blood, line her back. Her blowhole is clear of the water, but I cannot hear or see her breathe.

I take a step toward her. Her eye is partly open. The lids are dry and crusted with salt. The eye beneath looks dull and lifeless, like frosted glass. She doesn't blink or move.

I crouch down beside her in the sand. Strands of thick seaweed are wrapped around her lower jaw. Except as I look closer, it's not seaweed at all. It's fine mesh fishing net. Fine mesh nylon wrapped so tightly, it has cut deep into the skin behind her dolphin smile. Her tongue is blue-black and swollen. Shreds of nylon twist around her peglike teeth. Flies buzz up from the wound, and I see peck marks from the ravens around her jaw.

I sink down onto my knees and feel bile rising up inside me. I can see how she came to be like this. I can see her drowning, tangled in dark waters, thrashing in a fishing net trying to escape.

I close my eyes and try to push those thoughts away.

But the image of the dolphin drowning haunts me.

I splash water on my face and open my eyes.

The sun is bright white in the sky. A line of sweat trickles down my back beneath my shirt.

I don't want to be here anymore.

I stand up to leave. But I want to touch the dolphin once before I go.

I wet my fingers and reach out to trace them in an arc across her face.

17

"PFWHOOOSH!!"

I fall back into the water.

A blast of wet breath fills the air.

It stinks of fish.

The dolphin draws in a breath, a whistling sucking through her blowhole; then the blowhole snaps shut again.

The dolphin's eye is wide open now. She is watching me.

I slap the water with my hand. "You're alive!" I shout. "You're alive."

The dolphin's tail flukes flap the shallow water.

I get up and kneel down beside her, so my face is close to hers. I look into her small pale-pink eye. She blinks and looks back, as if she's working out just who I am and what I'm going to do.

But my mind is blank. All these years I've secretly dreamed of rescuing a dolphin, and now I don't know what to do. I put my hands on her side and try to roll her back to sea, but she might as well be one of the boulders on the shore. She's much too heavy on land. She breathes again, a sudden burst of air, and I wonder if I've hurt her by doing this.

I reach out to touch the white dolphin's face again. Her skin is dry and hard, like sunbaked rubber. I remember I have to keep her wet and shaded from the sun. All the things Mum taught me start flooding back. I know she could dehydrate out here. I jump up and run across the beach from boulder to boulder, pulling armfuls of wet seaweed from the

150

rocks. I lay these across her body, careful to keep her blowhole open and uncovered.

I dig hollows in the sand beneath her fins to take the pressure off the bones inside. Tiny sand-hoppers flip around the scooped-out sand. I brush my hair back from my eyes and see the white dolphin is still watching me.

I force myself to look at the wound in her mouth. The fishing net has cut deep into the skin. I try to gently pull the green mesh, unwinding it from around the teeth. Strands of fresh blood thread into the wet sand. The dolphin flinches as I pull and slaps her tail. Her tongue is a swollen mess. Her mouth is bruised, a bloody mass of skin and muscle. I can even see the white of jawbone shining through. She can't catch fish like this. Even if I wait with her until the tide turns and comes back in, I don't see how she can survive.

I scoop water with my hand and let it trail across her wounds. I don't know what to do. I just don't know what to do.

The mother has slipped back with the tide and is too far out to hear her call. The white dolphin's eyes close. I wait to hear her breathe. I count the seconds in my head, but the breath doesn't come. I don't know how long she can last like this.

"Wake up!" I shout. I tap my fingers on her side. She blasts air out through her blowhole. She opens her eye again and looks at me. She mustn't sleep. Dolphins don't sleep. I know that if she falls asleep, she'll die. I remember Mum telling me that every dolphin breath is a conscious thought. People don't have to think to breathe, but dolphins must remember to take each one. Dolphins suffering in captivity can choose not to breathe. They can choose to die.

And I don't want her to die.

I soak my coat in seawater and squeeze it out across her back. I keep talking to her all the time. I tell her that she will swim with her mother across the sea again.

She watches me closely as I clean sand from

around her eyes and mouth. I look into her small, pale eye and have the strangest feeling I am looking at myself. I wonder if she sees her own reflection in my world too.

I feel I'm keeping her alive somehow.

I know I must get help, but I can't leave her here all alone.

The ravens croak above me on the clifftop.

I press my head against hers and close my eyes.

I don't know what to do.

I just don't know what to do.

"KARA!"

I look up and fall backward in the wet sand.

Someone is stumbling up through the shallow waves toward me in a wet suit and fluorescent life jacket.

I can't believe it.

He's silhouetted against the sun, but I know just who it is.

"How did *you* get here?" I ask.

18

Felix stops in the shallow water and stares up at the sheer cliffs behind me. "I could ask you the same thing," he says. "I told Dad it was you here on the beach."

Beyond Felix, I see his dad swimming in from a small sailing dinghy anchored in the cove.

Felix sinks onto his knees beside the dolphin. "What happened here?"

I kneel down beside him. "She's been caught in fishing net."

"Is she alive?"

I nod. "Only just."

I hear Felix's dad's feet slap on the sand behind us. He crouches down beside the white dolphin. "There's another dolphin in the water going crazy," he says. "It almost caught my leg with its tail. I guess this must be its calf."

"We must get help," I say. "The Marine Life Rescue will help with this."

Felix's dad pulls his mobile from a waterproof pouch around his waist. He taps the keys and frowns. "No signal. It must be these cliffs."

"Can't we push her to the water?" asks Felix.

I shake my head. "She needs a vet anyway."

Felix's dad stands up and looks out toward the sailing dinghy. "Listen, I'll sail back and get some help. You two stay here with the dolphin."

"Go to the chandlery and ask for Carl," I say. "I think he works part-time there."

I watch Felix's dad climb into the dinghy and guide it out of the narrow cove. It's not like the dinghies at the sailing club. Felix's dad sits deep inside the center of the boat, like a racing driver in a car, instead of sitting at the stern next to the tiller.

I scoop some water from the trench around the dolphin's body and pour it through the layers of seaweed protecting her from the sun. "I thought you were going back to London."

Felix frowns. "What made you think that?"

"You weren't at school today and your dad didn't want to buy *Moana*. He said he was going to listen to what you wanted instead."

Felix helps scoop more water and runs his wet hand along the dolphin's skin. "Dad *did* listen to me," he says. "That sailing yesterday was the coolest thing I've ever done, but I can't sail a boat like *Moana* by myself. I like to be the one in control, remember?"

"So?" I say.

Felix sits back in the sand and grins. "So Dad borrowed a sailing dinghy from someone he knows through the cerebral palsy charity. I couldn't believe it when they brought it over today. That's why I didn't come into school. Dad and I decided to try it out in the bay. It's designed for the Paralympics. The seat is low down in the cockpit, and I can control the sails and tiller with a central joystick with just one arm."

"So you're really going to learn to sail?" I say.

Felix grins. "Not just that. I'm going to win the regatta race around Gull Rock in five weeks' time."

I flick water at him. "You'll be in second place. *Moana*'s going to win it this year. She always does."

Felix flicks water back at me and laughs. "I wouldn't bet on that if I were you."

We hear the rescue boat before we see it. The orange rib inflatable boat slews in a narrow arc into the cove with the dolphin mother arching through its bow waves. Dad and Mr. Andersen are sitting in the boat with two Marine Life Rescue volunteers. One I recognize as Carl, one of Mum's marine biology students from last year, and the other, Greg, one of the local crab potters and scallop divers.

Carl switches off the engine, drops a shallow anchor in the water, and jumps out of the boat. He runs up the sun-bright sand toward us. I haven't seen him since the night we floated candles out to sea for Mum. He used to make amazing sand sculptures of mermaids and sea monsters just for me.

I pull him down beside me. "You have to save her, Carl," I say.

Carl kneels down and pulls some weed away from the dolphin's head and whistles softly. "She's albino. I've never seen an albino dolphin before."

"She's badly injured," I say. "She needs a vet."

"We've called the vet, but she's out on another emergency right now," he says. He shines a small pocket flashlight inside her mouth. "You're right. These wounds are nasty."

"But how long will the vet be?" I don't think the dolphin will last much longer here.

"She said she'd radio us when she's on her way," he says.

Mr. Andersen, Greg, and Dad join us.

Dad crouches down beside me. "Mr. Andersen told me you were here. You know you're not meant to come here on your own."

"I'm sorry, Dad," I say. "But if I hadn't come . . ."

Dad sighs and shakes his head. "You can't just go running off. I have to know where you are."

"I will, Dad, next time . . ."

"Hold this," says Carl. He passes me the end of a tape measure. "You stand at the head end, Kara. You don't want to be in the way of her tail."

We measure the dolphin from beak to tail flukes. Carl reaches into the black bag for a clipboard and a pen. "Sixty-five inches," he says. "She can't be much more than a year old. She may even still be feeding from her mother."

Felix points toward the water. "Her mother's out there, waiting for her."

Carl nods and writes notes on his clipboard. "We saw her as we came in."

Greg crouches down to examine the white dolphin too. He presses his hand against her flanks.

159

When he takes it away, it leaves a dented handprint in her skin. He shakes his head. "Not a good sign. She's very dehydrated."

Carl looks at his watch. "Her breathing rate is up too. Ten breaths a minute. It should be about four or five." He sits back on his heels and rubs his chin.

I wet my fingers and trace water across the white dolphin's face. She blinks and watches me. "What are we going to do, Carl?"

Carl runs his hands through his hair. "Let's give her some fluids by stomach tube while we wait for the vet to get here."

Greg nods. "It'll make her feel better. But I don't think there'll be much the vet can do."

I feel my mouth go dry. "What d'you mean, not much she can do?"

Carl looks at Greg and then at me. He talks softly to try to break the news, but it makes no difference, the words are still the same. "These wounds are bad, Kara. She can't catch fish like this, and I doubt she could suckle from her mother. She would die if we let her go back to sea."

He reaches in the bag and pulls out a long clear tube.

"You mean the vet will put her down?" I say.

Carl looks up and nods. "I'm sorry, Kara. I don't think she'll have a choice."

I stand up and back away from him. "But her mother's waiting for her."

Dad wraps his arms around me. "I know it's hard, but Carl's right. It'd be cruel to put her back into the sea."

I push Dad's hands away and glare at Carl.

Carl crouches down next to the white dolphin's head and looks up at me. "You've done really well, Kara. Both you and Felix, you've done everything right."

I scowl at him. "It's made no difference."

"It has to her," he says. "She's suffered less because of you."

I watch Carl measure the stomach tube against the dolphin's side and then slide it into her mouth. She shakes her head as it passes over her swollen tongue.

"You're hurting her," I say.

Carl doesn't speak or take his eyes off the dolphin until the tube is pushed in place. He stands up and holds the bag of fluids high. I watch the level sink lower in the bag as the fluids pass through and into her. I just stand and stare at him. I can't believe it's come to this, that there is nothing else they can do.

Carl glances at Greg. "Why don't you take these guys back to the harbor? You can pick the vet up from there too when she arrives."

"I'm not leaving," I say.

Felix sits back and digs his hand deep into the sand. "I'm staying too."

Carl presses his head against the bag of fluids. "You won't want to stay."

"Come on, Kara," says Dad. He tucks his hand under my arm. "I think it's for the best."

"You too, Felix," says Mr. Andersen. "You've done all you can do."

I pull away from Dad and kneel down beside the

white dolphin and stroke her head. She watches me so closely that I can't help thinking she wants our help. I know she doesn't want to die.

I look up at Carl. "There must be *something* we can do."

Felix kneels down beside her too. "Why can't we take her to a rescue center, where they can look after her until she's better? They do it in America."

"We don't have sea life centers here," says Carl. "Even if we did, they might not take her, because wild animals can pass on diseases to the captive ones."

"What about a swimming pool?" asks Felix. "Or one of those small inflatable pools you can buy?"

I nod. "Felix is right. There's got to be something like that we could use."

Carl drops the bag of fluids lower and sighs. "Look, kids, it's no use. Even if we could use someone's swimming pool, it wouldn't be right for a dolphin. For a start, a swimming pool is full of chemicals and has fresh water, not salt water. The water would need to be changed and filtered to get rid of waste. Forget it. We don't have salt water pools in this country. We don't have anything like that."

I jump up to my feet. "But we do, Carl!" I almost shout the words out. "We have something *exactly* like that."

19

"The Blue Pool?" asks Carl.

I nod. "You know; the tidal pool out toward the headland. It's perfect. The sea washes over it and cleans it out twice a day."

"I don't know," says Carl. "I mean, if the weather gets rough, there can be big waves crashing over there. We can't have rescuers putting their own lives at risk."

I look up at the clear, blue sky. "The forecast is

good for this week," I say. "Please, Carl, we have to chance it."

Carl looks at Greg, and he shrugs his shoulders.

"Seems like it'd be worth a go to me," says Mr. Andersen.

"We've got to try," says Felix.

Carl sighs. He gently slides the stomach tube out of the dolphin. It slithers out, smeared with blood and slime. "I'll radio the vet, see what she thinks."

I watch Carl walk down the sloping beach to the rescue boat. I pick up scoopfuls of dry sand and let it trickle through my fingers. Carl speaks into the radio. I try to read his face, but all I see is him nod and frown. Felix crosses the fingers of his good hand and holds them up to me. I smile, but I don't feel much hope inside. Carl is walking back toward us, his face grim and serious.

I jump up and brush the sand from my clothes. "What did she say?"

Carl shakes his head. "The vet thinks the stress of moving the dolphin may be too much."

"It's her only chance," Felix blurts out.

"I know," says Carl, "and the vet can't get to us for at least another hour. Considering the injuries, she thinks it might be worth trying your plan and taking the dolphin to the tidal pool so she can assess it there."

"Thank you, Carl." I grin. "She'll get better now. I know she will."

Carl shakes his head. "She's very sick. Don't get your hopes up too much."

Carl fetches a tarpaulin from the rescue boat, and I help to slide the edges to the dolphin's sides.

"When we roll her on," instructs Carl, "watch out for her tail. Keep away from her blowhole too. Their breath can carry some nasty diseases."

We all line up and put our hands on the dolphin's back.

"This is the risky part," says Carl. "Her lungs have been crushed by the weight of her own body. She could find it difficult to breathe."

Carl nods the signal, and we all push and tilt her to one side. Greg slides the tarpaulin under her, and we roll her the other way and pull the sheet out straight beneath her. The dolphin lashes her tail against the sand. Already she seems stronger from the fluids. Her flippers and tail have lost their deep blue color, and have gained a tinge of pink. Carl rubs Vaseline around her blowhole and spreads sunblock onto her body as Greg wipes the tarpaulin clear of grit and sand.

I take a corner of the tarpaulin with Dad. The dolphin is much heavier than I thought she would be, and we struggle with her to the water's edge. Greg pulls the rescue boat close up to the shore, and we heave her in. She takes up most of the space inside the boat, and the rest of us have to sit out on the rubber sides. I pull on a spare life jacket and cling on as Carl fires up the engines and takes the boat out of the cove and into the wind and waves and sea.

The mother dolphin follows us, almost pressed against the boat, lifting her head above the water to see her calf. She whistles and clicks to her and slaps her tail down hard. I wonder what she is trying to say and if she understands what we are trying to do.

"She's injured too," I say.

Carl shades his eyes against the sun. A deep V-shaped notch is cut into the base of her dorsal fin. The edges are raw and congealed with blood. "I don't think it's as bad as it looks," he says. "It's superficial. It should heal okay."

He slows down as we enter the harbor walls. "I can't take her to the tidal pool," he says. "There are too many rocks at low tide. We'll have to take her across land from here."

The mother dolphin follows us, her dorsal fin curving through the water, as if she's on a towrope right behind. She's still with us, despite the smell of oil and diesel in the harbor and the outboard engine roar that must echo underwater between the walls.

The tide is low, and I feel the underside of the boat scrape on the mud and stones. Carl pulls up at the bottom of the slipway where the concrete is barnacled and green with seaweed and algae.

"I'll get my pickup truck," says Greg. "We'll drive her across to the Blue Pool."

Carl nods. He wets a cloth and lets the water trickle across the white dolphin's back. The mother dolphin surfaces in the deeper water and blasts a breath of air. The white dolphin copies its mother, the *pfwhooosh* of their breaths calling each other, letting each other know they are still there.

"How will she know where we're taking her calf?" I ask Carl.

He shrugs his shoulders. "That's why this might not be a good idea. The separation stress could be too much for her."

I see Greg's truck reversing down the slipway. Two other Marine Life Rescue volunteers jog alongside. Greg slams his driver's door and unhooks the tailgate of the pickup. "The vet's waiting at the tidal pool for us," he says. "There are other volunteers there too."

"Good." Carl nods. "Let's get her there."

Carl helps Felix climb out of the boat, and I join

Felix on the slipway. We stand back to let the rescue volunteers lift the white dolphin up into the truck. She lies on foam mattresses sandwiched between Greg's crab pots and folded nets.

Carl turns to Dad and Mr. Andersen, and nods in our direction. "I think you should take these kids home," he says. "They both need to get warm and dry."

"I'm fine," I say. I tuck my hands under my armpits to warm them up and hide the blueness of my fingers. My feet are numb with cold.

"I'm fine too," says Felix.

Mr. Andersen puts his arm around Felix. "Look at you. You're shivering. You're freezing cold."

I put my foot on the tow bar. I want to climb up beside the white dolphin and go with her to the tidal pool. "I've got to come with you, Carl," I say.

Carl puts his hand across to stop me. "Not this time," he says. "The vet will need time to assess her and make her decision."

"I have to come."

Carl hauls himself up beside the white dolphin.

"I'll ring your dad tonight. I'll let you know what happens."

Greg revs the truck and the white dolphin thrashes her tail and blasts air through her blowhole.

I hold onto the tailgate. "Don't let her die, Carl. Please don't let the vet her put down."

Carl looks down and shakes his head. "It won't be up to me, Kara."

I put my hands on the dolphin's face and look into her eye. But she looks beyond me to her mother and the blue curve of the horizon far beyond the harbor walls.

Carl pulls on my hands. "Let go, Kara."

I lift my hands and watch the truck drive up the slipway and disappear into the traffic along the harbor road.

I hate it. I hate them taking her away from her mother like this. I feel as if I'm betraying her some-how.

It feels worse than letting her take her chances in the sea.

20

Daisy spreads a white bun thick with jam. "Are we going to see the dolphin?"

I put my fingers to my lips. Aunt Bev is making a pot of tea. "We'll have to go now," I whisper, "before school."

Daisy nods and bolts down her roll.

Last night she sat wide-eyed while I told her all about the dolphin. She'd scowled when I told her Felix had been there to help too. I told her that he was all right really, that he'd been angry the day we'd met him in the café. But it didn't seem to matter what I said about Felix. Daisy's made her mind up about him already.

I sling my schoolbag over my shoulder and wait for Daisy by the door.

Aunt Bev narrows her eyes at me. "You're off early."

"Got some homework to hand in," I say.

She stares hard at me and Daisy. "You're not planning on seeing that dolphin, are you?"

I shrug my shoulders. "What dolphin?" I glance at Daisy, but she's turned bright red and is staring at the floor.

Aunt Bev folds her arms. "The one Jim was talking about on the phone after you two had gone to bed."

"What did he say?"

"I don't know," says Aunt Bev. "I didn't hear all of it."

"I just want to know if it's all right," I say.

174

"You're both going straight to school. You've been in enough trouble as it is, and I don't want Daisy in trouble too." She grabs her handbag and the door keys. "In fact, I'll walk you there myself."

There's no point arguing with her. Dad's on an early shift at work, so I can't ask him.

All the way to school I try to catch glimpses of the headland, but the tidal pool is tucked away below the cliffs and out of sight. Greg's pickup truck is parked in the headland parking lot, so all I can do is hope that means Greg and Carl are there and that the dolphin is still alive.

I can't concentrate on anything all day. Felix has been moved to the top group in math and English, so I only get a chance to meet up with him at break.

He's talking to two girls from our year at the tuckshop, but he breaks away from them when he sees me. I sit down next to him on one of the wooden benches in the playground. "How's the dolphin?"

Felix fumbles with a chocolate wrapper and tears the corner with his teeth. "Carl rang to say she's still alive," he says. "They need volunteers to support her on a raft until she can balance on her own in the water. Dad's doing a two-hour shift before he picks me up at lunch."

"I could meet you there later, when I get out of school," I say. "Maybe Carl will let us help too."

"Yeah, that'd be cool," says Felix. He snaps the chocolate and offers me some. "At my last school you could get expelled for eating chocolate."

I stuff two chunks of chocolate in my mouth. "No way!"

Felix grins. "Chocolate was forbidden. We were only allowed cereal bars and carrot sticks for snacks." He shoves the rest of the bar in his mouth and speaks through a mouthful of chocolate. "I think I could get to like it here."

After lunch I watch the hands on the clock above the teacher's desk turn slowly around and around and around. I'm jealous that Felix will be at the Blue Pool already. When the end-of-school bell rings, I'm first out of the gates. I run to Daisy's school and grab her when I see her. I almost pull her down the road. I can't wait to see the dolphin. "Come on." I sling her bag across my shoulder. "We've got to run."

The tide is too high to walk along the sand to the Blue Pool, so I run with Daisy along the coastal road. The headland parking lot is now full of cars, but Greg's pickup has gone. There are lots of people too, strung out along the coastal path. A crowd has gathered on the cliff above the tidal pool. I guess news has spread quickly about the dolphin. I push my way through the people to the stone steps down to the pool, but a line of police tape is stretched across the path, and a policewoman puts her arm across to stop me from going through.

"No one's allowed," she says, "I'm sorry."

I glance down to the rocks. Two dome tents stand on the ledge of flat rocks above the pool. I can see rucksacks and sleeping bags piled up inside. A white cover stands on poles, stretched across the pool to shelter the dolphin from the sun. Only her tail sticks out beyond the cover. She lies supported on a flotation raft between two long yellow cushions of air. A woman I've not seen before crouches next to a small gas stove and pours steaming water from a kettle into two mugs. Behind her, towels and wet suits are draped across the rocks to dry.

"I have to go down there," I say.

The policewoman shakes her head and smiles. "I can't let you I'm afraid."

"Carl!" I yell. "Carl, it's me."

She tries to gently push me back, but I see Carl's head pop out from under the white cover.

He speaks to someone in the pool and runs up the stone steps toward me. His feet leave dark, wet prints on the pale rock. He ducks under the police tape and pulls Daisy and me away from the crowd.

My words tumble out. "How is she?"

Carl sits us down on the grassy verge. "She's holding her own for now," he says. "But she can't swim. Her muscles have been damaged from all that time she spent pressed against the sand."

"Why can't we see her?" Daisy asks.

Carl glances back at the crowd. "The vet said the dolphin could pass some diseases onto people. But it's for the dolphin's protection too. We've got volunteers camped here for shifts in the water, but we don't want lots of people trying to touch her. She needs peace and quiet."

"But *we* can see her, can't we?" I ask. "It was me who found her. We can help look after her."

Carl shakes his head and sighs. He runs his hands through his hair. "Kara, I don't know how to tell you this, but it's not good news."

My hands feel clammy and cold. Daisy clutches my arm. "What?" I ask.

"The vet has taken advice from some experts in America. Even if we can make her better, she won't survive in the wild without other dolphins. She's far too young."

I point toward the harbor. "But her mother's waiting for her," I say.

179

Carl frowns. "Lots of boats went out to ride alongside her. We haven't seen her for several hours now. We think she's been scared away."

"She'll come back, though," I say. "Won't she?"

Carl shrugs his shoulders. "She last saw her calf in the harbor. She doesn't even know her calf is here."

"We can't give up now, Carl. We'll look for her."

Carl peels his wet-suit gloves off and rubs his eyes. His chin is covered in fine stubble. He looks exhausted. I guess he's been up all night. "Felix and his dad are sailing in the bay looking for her right now," he says. "But she could be miles away. She might have even rejoined her pod."

I stand up and kick the ground. "So how long do we give the mother to come back? A week? Two weeks? A year?"

Carl breathes out softly through his teeth. "Tomorrow. The vet says we'll give her until tomorrow."

"Tomorrow?" I shout. "You can't do that. She'll come back, I know she will." Heads start to turn our way, but I don't care.

Carl leans forward and lowers his voice. "It's not

fair to put her calf through this if we can't release her to the wild. It's not up to me, Kara. Many stranded whales and dolphins die or need to be put down. It's not easy, but it's just the way it is."

I glare at him. "At least let me see her."

"I can't, Kara," he says. "I'm sorry. I just can't."

He squeezes my shoulder, but I pull away from him. I storm across the parking lot and sink down behind a stone wall, out of sight.

Daisy slides down and puts her arms around me. "What are you going to do?"

I push my palms against my eyes and shake my head. "I don't know, Daisy," I say. "I just don't know." I feel so helpless sitting here. There's absolutely nothing I can do.

I watch a jackdaw strut up and down beside us, its beady blue eyes on a crust of bread beside my feet. I pick the bread up and roll it between my finger and thumb into a small ball of dough. "I wish Mum was here," I say. "She'd tell me what to do."

The jackdaw hops forward. It turns its head from side to side, watching me all the time.

I hold the bread out on the flat of my hand.

I wonder if it will dare. I wonder if it will dare to put its trust in me.

Daisy slips her hand in mine. "Maybe there's a way you *can* ask her."

I turn to Daisy and nod.

I was thinking exactly the same thing too.

21

A small, blue memory stick, molded in the shape of a dolphin. Mum brought it back from a conference about sea life, and I always wanted it for my own. I took it from her room the day before she left, just because I liked it. I never told her, and I feel guilty about it still. After she disappeared, I threaded it onto a necklace made of shells. It now hangs below the pure-white cowrie shell I found. The other shells are top shells, the purple stripes worn away to show the pearliness beneath, and between each of these a periwinkle, sunshine yellow.

I run along the seafront with Daisy, clutching the only thing I have of Mum's in my hand. It's all I've got. She never kept *things*. She didn't even want a wedding ring from Dad. She had her diving kit and camera, and that was all. The computer wasn't even hers. It belonged to the research center. The only *thing* she kept was her old, battered green rucksack. The rips were patched with different fabrics from different lands. Each patch of cloth told a different story, she used to say. But that rucksack is now gone. It went with her, too.

I know I haven't got long. Aunt Bev gave me money to get fish and chips for supper and will expect us back in half an hour. I leave Daisy in the queue. It's a long one that snakes around the corner and along the harbor road. It'll buy me some time at least. I turn up past the chandlery and jog up the steep hill out of the other side of town. My legs ache and my lungs hurt when I breathe, but I don't stop until I reach the row of whitewashed cottages overlooking the sea.

Miss Penluna's cottage stands at the end, along a shared gravel pathway. The stones scrunch under my feet as I walk past the other doorways. Buckets and spades, and bodyboards lie outside in the small front gardens. Window boxes bright with geraniums sit on the slate window ledges. No one *real* lives in these cottages anymore. They're all holiday rentals now.

All except the end house. Miss Penluna's cottage is a pale off-white gray. Beneath the flaking whitewash, the stones are dry and crumbly. The windows are smeared with windblown sea salt from past winter storms and the curtains behind are drawn tightly shut. In the tangle of weeds and grasses in front of the cottage stands a lone bird feeder filled with seed. It's the only clue that someone lives in here at all.

I stand in front of the door. My heart is banging in my chest. I can feel it pulse through me and against the memory stick I have clutched in my hand.

I lift my hand and knock on the door.

Something scrabbles against the other side. Then all is still. I knock again. Maybe Miss Penluna has gone out to feed the gulls again.

I slowly turn the handle of the door. It creaks and the door pushes inward. A blade of sunlight cuts through the darkness to a flagstone floor.

"Hello?" I call.

The cottage is silent. I take a step inside and almost gag. A sharp stench fills my nose and mouth and stings my eyes. It smells of the cliffs at Gull Rock when the cliffs are covered with birds at breeding time.

"Shut the door!"

A flurry of feathers beats against my face, and the door slams shut. In the gloom, I see the small figure of Miss Penluna standing in front of me.

"You can't take him," she says. "He's not well."

"Take who?" I say.

She peers at me closely. "You from the council?"

"I'm Kara. We met on the beach."

I hear the scrape of claws on the flagstones

beside me and watch a jackdaw hop away toward another door.

"You can't stay," Miss Penluna says. She shakes her head and points with her stick to the door. "You've got to go."

"I need your help," I say.

"Off you go." She opens the door and tries to prod me out.

"Please," I say. "I need your help."

She stops still, the end of her stick against my chest.

"I've got something to show the angels."

Miss Penluna peers outside, then grasps my arms in her bony hand, and shuts the door. "You can't stay long."

I follow her into the kitchen. The floor is strewn with newspaper and empty china plates. The jackdaw flaps and hops on the table and watches me with its bright blue eyes.

"So what do you want to know?" she says.

I twirl the shell necklace around and around my hand. "Can you really talk to angels?"

Miss Penluna pushes a chair out from under the table with her stick and sits down. "They think I'm mad down in the village."

I pull out another chair and sit opposite her at the table. The white tablecloth is splattered with patterns of spilled tea and jackdaw droppings.

She reaches out a bony finger and gently strokes the bird across its beak. "I've always heard them singing in my head. My mother told me they were angels." She sits back and shakes her head. "I don't hear them so much anymore."

I slide the necklace and dolphin memory stick across the table. "This belongs to my mother," I say.

Miss Penluna turns it over in her hand. Her fingers are long and thin. Clawlike almost. She pulls the memory stick apart and peers at the metal USB drive inside. "What's this?" she asks.

"A memory stick," I say.

She holds it close up to her eyes. "Whose memories?"

"It's not like that," I say. "It's for a computer." I wonder if Miss Penluna has even seen a computer before.

She clips it shut and brushes it aside to the edge of the table. Maybe it's not good enough to show her. She's not interested in it at all. The jackdaw tries to peck at it, so I put it in my lap and wait.

Miss Penluna leans forward on the table. "What is it you *really* want to know?"

My mouth goes dry. My mind is blank. I close my eyes and try to think.

The jackdaw's feet tip tap on the table.

"I want to know what happened," I say. "I want to know what happened the night Mum disappeared."

When I open my eyes, Miss Penluna is still watching me. She pushes her wispy hair from her face. "The question is, are you ready?"

I grip the memory stick tightly in my hand and nod. I'm about to know what happened. I'm about to know the truth. I feel like I am standing on a cliff edge looking down, and I feel I am about to fall.

"You must listen to the dolphins," says Miss Penluna.

I shake my head and stare at her. I thought I'd hear an answer, a definite answer. "I don't know what you mean," I say.

Miss Penluna shrugs her shoulders. "They are angels of the sea."

I sit back. I feel cheated somehow, as if I've used up my magic question and now other questions are flooding in my head too. How can I save the white dolphin? How can I stop the dredgers ripping up the bay? Will I ever see Mum again?

Miss Penluna leans forward and grasps both my hands in hers. I notice her eyes are pale, pale blue, just like the jackdaw.

"You will hear her if you listen," she says. "You must listen to the dolphins."

22

By the time I reach the chip shop, I can see Daisy through the window handing over money to the man behind the counter. I lean on the railings, catch my breath, and look down into the dark green harbor water. It's almost low tide. Mooring ropes lie long and draped with seaweed. I was stupid to build my hopes up and think I would find some answers. I don't even know how to save the white dolphin. Aunt Bev is right. Miss Penluna is mad. She's as mad as they come. Mum never believed in talking dolphins, not with human voices anyway.

Daisy hands me the bag, hot with packets of fish and chips. "What did the Bird Lady say?"

"Later," I say. "Come on, let's get home."

"Don't look now," says Daisy. She nudges me in the ribs.

I look beyond her to see Felix and his dad walking toward us on the pavement. They're both wearing wet suits and life jackets. Their legs are caked in mud.

Felix and his dad stop beside us. I wrinkle my nose. Their wet suits smell of rotten seaweed.

"We got caught out by the tide." Mr. Andersen smiles. "I guess we've got a lot to learn."

Daisy pulls my arm, trying to hide behind me. I elbow her away and turn to Felix. "Did you see the mother dolphin?"

Felix shakes his head. "We went past Gull Rock and farther up the coast, but we didn't see any sign of her."

I twist the necklace through my fingers. The mother dolphin could be anywhere by now. "She must be somewhere out there."

"We saw grey seals," says Felix, "and a basking shark, a huge one . . ."

"She wouldn't leave her calf," I say. I twist the silk thread of the necklace around and around and around. Daisy grabs my arm again. She yanks it back and the silk breaks, scattering shells across the ground. "DAISY!" I yell. I scrabble on the floor to save the shells, but some bounce over the harbor edge. I look down to see the cowrie shell plop into the water, spreading green ripples in circle patterns of light.

I spin around to look for the memory stick, but that's gone too. I didn't even see it drop into the water. I look inside the bag with the fish and chips to see if it fell in there.

Daisy holds out three periwinkles and a top shell in her hand. "I'm sorry, Kara." Her eyes are welling with tears.

I scoop them from her hand. They're all that's left.

"Is this yours?" Felix is crouching down, his hands in the gutter. "I thought this dropped too."

He straightens up and holds out the blue dolphin memory stick in his hand.

"Thanks," I say. I curl my fingers around it and slide it in my pocket.

He frowns at me. "I thought you weren't into computers."

"I'm not." I hold it tightly in my hand. "It's Mum's."

"What's on it?"

I shrug my shoulders. "I think it's empty." I don't want to tell him that I tried looking on the school computer, but I couldn't read the log-in signs. I showed Carl once too, but he said it was password locked.

"I could take a look," says Felix. "If there's something on there, I'll find it."

I run my finger along the curved dolphin shape in my pocket. I've always wondered if there was anything on there, some photos of Mum, a diary? I've always wanted to know. "Maybe," I say.

"I'll look after it," he says. "Promise."

I press the memory stick deeper into my pocket. "It's all I have."

"Up to you," Felix says. "But let me know if you change your mind."

I watch him follow his dad along the seafront. I know I won't find out any other way.

"Wait," I call after him.

He turns back to me.

I hold the memory stick out to him. "I want you to," I say. "I want you to look."

Felix nods, and I place it in his outstretched hand.

Maybe that's exactly what it is.

Memories.

Someone's memories, waiting to be unlocked.

We're late getting home with the fish and chips. Aunt Bev is in her robe, stretched out on the sofa, watching a talent show on TV. Her stomach's so big now that I wonder how she doesn't burst.

Daisy puts plates out on the table. "I'm sorry about your necklace."

I scatter forks across the table. "Doesn't matter."

"What did she say?" asks Daisy. "What did the Bird Lady say?"

I thump the ketchup in the middle. "She said the dolphins were the angels of the sea."

Daisy stops, plate in hand. "Real angels?"

"Don't be silly, Daisy," I snap. I rip open the grease-spotted paper of the fish and chip packets. "They're just dolphins. Animals, like us."

Dad sits down at the table and yawns. Dark rings sit under his eyes. He's doing as many hours as he can at the pub. I hardly see him these days at all. He picks up a fat chip and takes a bite.

Aunt Bev and Daisy sit down too.

"Tom's home tomorrow," Aunt Bev says. "Let's hope they've had a good catch this time."

I see Daisy's eyes light up. "He said he'd take me to see a film."

I shake salt on to my chips. I don't want to see what tomorrow brings. I turn to Dad. "Can we go sailing before school?"

Dad shakes his head. "I'm on three shifts."

"But we have to look for the mother dolphin," I say. "We have to find her. Her calf will be put down if we don't."

Dad wipes his mouth with a napkin. "Look, Kara, Carl's been out there looking today and so have Mr. Andersen and Felix."

"But we know the bay better than any of them. We'll find her."

Dad puts the napkin down and pushes his plate away. "I haven't got time tomorrow."

I stab a chip with my fork. "You've never got time anymore."

Dad glares at me. "That's not fair, Kara. I have to earn some money."

"But we have to find her, Dad."

Dad gets up and chucks the chip paper in the bin. "It's the ocean, for God's sake, Kara. She could be anywhere. How would we know where to look?"

I push my plate away. "You've given up, like everyone else."

Aunt Bev rests her hand on my arm. "Listen to your father, Kara."

I push my chair back and ignore Aunt Bev. "You've given up," I yell at Dad. "Like you've given up on Mum." I storm up to the room I share with Daisy. I lie down on the cot fully clothed and pull the covers over my head. Dad comes in the room and whispers my name, but I pretend to be asleep. I hear the bang of the front door as he leaves the house and the blare of the TV in the room below.

When Daisy comes into the bedroom, I wait for her to put out the light and settle down in bed. When I hear her steady breathing, I fold the covers back and look up through the window at the darkening sky.

"Kara?"

I hold my breath. I thought she was asleep.

"I know you're awake," she whispers.

I let my breath out slowly and turn on my side.

"Where is she?" Daisy asks. "Where do you think she is?"

I feel silent tears fall down my face and soak into my pillow. "I don't know," I say. "I just don't know."

23

The sun is bright, bright white.

The sea is turquoise blue.

I sit on the shoreline scooping sand to make a moat around my castle. It's the perfect castle. Three tall turrets and a drawbridge made from driftwood. I've decorated it with shells and seaweed. A cowrie shell reflects the sunlight from the turret nearest the sea. I fold my arms around my knees and gaze at it. Nothing can knock my castle down. But I don't hear the wave. It swirls into the moat and floods the castle walls. The turret nearest the sea is the first to fall. It slumps into the waves and disappears. The cowrie shell rolls along the hard, wet sand toward the sea. I try to scoop it up, but it slips through my fingers and tumbles into foaming surf.

"Come on in, Kara."

Mum is standing in the water, smiling. The wind blows back her hair. I can even see the freckles on her face and the sunlight in her gray-green eyes. She's wearing the T-shirt and cut-off jeans she always wears. A wave furls around her legs and rushes up the sand toward me.

Mum shades her eyes against the sun. "Come *on*, Kara." She smiles. "I'm waiting for you."

It's bright, bright white, that sun.

The waves are sliding on the shore, in and out, in and out.

But I want to find that cowrie shell. I search through seaweed heaped upon the sand, but all I find are beer-can rings and plastic bottle tops.

I look back out to sea.

But Mum has gone.

The moon is shining through the window, bright, bright white.

Daisy is breathing softly in her bed, in and out, in and out.

But I just stare at the bright white moon.

I saw Mum's face. I heard her voice.

I'm waiting for you.

It felt so real.

I reach under my cot for my swimming bag. Daisy snuffles in her sleep and turns on her side. The hands of her fairy clock point way past midnight. I grab my thick fleece, tiptoe down the stairs, and slip out into the night.

I have to find the dolphin.

I have to find a way to talk to Mum.

The night is still. I stand at the water's edge, scrunching my toes into the soft, damp sand. There are no waves. The high tide is slack, about to turn. The sea lies slick and black, like oil. I pull on my mask and fins and step into the water. I slide my feet forward until I stand waist deep. The cold water presses against my skin, but I feel strangely far away, as if my body isn't mine at all.

I dive under, wrapped in darkness. I feel I can dive farther and deeper tonight, as if I am part of the ocean, as if it's part of me. I run my hands along the rippled sand beneath me and listen to the deep, still silence. I hold my breath. The seconds stretch like hours. My heartbeat slows. My mind drifts, clear and light. Bright stars swirl through the water. Something is swimming with me, by my side. A dolphin. Her body glows bright white, shining in the darkness. A trail of spinning stars spiral from her fins and tail flukes.

She looks not of this world.

An underwater angel almost.

I take a breath, and she surfaces beside me.

"Pfwhooosh!"

I see the smooth dark curve of the dolphin's back and the deep notch in her dorsal fin, silhouetted in the moonlight. I knew the white dolphin's mother

would return. I knew she would come back here to the bay. She dives under again, leaving a tumbling trail of phosphorescent swirls of light. I dive too, and watch the bright stars trail from my fingertips. A million tiny plankton lighting up an underwater sky.

We surface again, and she swims around me. I hear her clicks and whistles and feel her sonar pulse right through me, reading me. Her small, dark eyes twinkle in the moonlight. I can hardly breathe. She is close, so close. I reach my hand out, and she lets me touch the smooth, warm skin of her face.

She dives again, and circles. I know she is looking for her calf, here in the shallow water. If she follows me along the shoreline to the Blue Pool, I can lead her there.

I keep close to the line of darks rocks that run out toward the headland, leaving the orange lights of town behind. The ebbing tide swirls around my legs, and I can feel its pull toward the open sea. I shouldn't be out here. Dad would kill me if he knew. I can almost hear his voice . . . *What'd you think you're doing, Kara? . . . Hypothermia . . . No life jacket . . . On your own too!* I shut him out and swim on, grasping on the barnacled rocks that graze my skin.

The sound of a car alarm and the rumble of a distant truck, carry out across the sea, reaching far into the night. But they belong to another world almost, not mine.

Everything seems farther at night. I think I've passed the Blue Pool when I see a light up ahead and two dome tents reflected in the moonlight.

Even at high tide, the water below the tidal pool is shallow and strewn with rocks. But now the tide is on the ebb, I can see the concrete rim of the pool above the water. I don't know if the mother dolphin can swim close enough to see her calf.

"Pfwhooosh!" The mother dolphin surfaces and lifts her head above the water.

I cling onto a rock and listen in the silence.

Then I hear another "Pfwhooosh" reply.

The mother dolphin slaps her tail, the sound echoing out across the water. She opens her beak, and a stream of whistles and clicks call out into the night.

Another blast of breath in the tidal pool calls out.

I hear voices from the pool too, human voices.

"Hey, Greg." It's Carl's voice. He must be on a night shift. "Something's out there."

I back away into rock shadows. I don't want Carl to see me here. He's silhouetted on the poolside, looking down into the water.

"There's another dolphin," calls Carl. "Get my flashlight. Let's see if it's the mother."

A beam of light scans the water and finds the dolphin. It follows the curve of her back to the deep notch in her dorsal fin.

"It's her all right," says Greg.

"Kara was right." Carl's voice is almost a whisper.

I strain my ears to hear the rest.

"She knew the mother dolphin would never stop looking until she found her calf."

24

"Wake up, Kara! Wake up!"

I feel small fingers poking at my eyelids.

"Wake up! You've missed breakfast. It's time for school."

I open my eyes and push the hands away. Daisy's sitting on my cot, staring at me.

"You've been asleep for ages," she says.

I push myself up. My head is fogged with sleep and my legs ache with cold, deep into the bone. My mind swirls with last night's dream.

Daisy reaches out her hand. "Why's your hair wet?"

I run my hand across my hair and see the dark patch on my pillow. My clothes lie in a wet heap on the floor. I was really there last night. I really saw the dolphin. It wasn't just a dream.

I swing my legs out of bed. "The mother dolphin is back. I saw her last night."

"You *saw* her?" Daisy's eyes are open wide.

I hold both her hands in mine. "Don't tell your mum, Daisy. Please don't tell."

I pull my school clothes on, grab my bag, and race down to the kitchen.

Aunt Bev is frying bacon on the stove. She tuts when she sees me. "You'll have to take a bacon sandwich with you on the way to school."

I take a slice of bread from the open packet on the table.

Uncle Tom is sitting at the table. He's in his shirt and oilskin trousers, the braces straps hang loose around his waist. He's unshaven and tired. He slumps forward and puts his head in his hands.

"Put the kettle on, Kara," says Aunt Bev. "Make your uncle a coffee."

I fill the kettle with cold water from the tap. Daisy tries to climb onto Uncle Tom's knee, but he pulls her off. "Get ready for school, Daisy. Don't be late."

He says it roughly, not like Uncle Tom at all. I pour boiling water into the mug and watch the powdered coffee swirl around. Aunt Bev is watching him. This is when he brings the money home, his share from selling all the fish they've caught at sea.

Uncle Tom sits back and opens his hands. His palms are bare. "There's nothing, Bev," he says. "French and Spanish boats were working the same area. We spent more on fuel than what we caught. Dougie Evans blames me. He says if I can't find fish for him, he'll find another skipper for his boat."

"He can't do that, Tom! We got bills to pay, and the baby's due soon." Aunt Bev glances in my direction. "We've extra mouths to feed, too."

"I know that, Bev, I know."

"Tom, we *need* the money."

Uncle Tom slams his hands on the table. "What d'you think I'm trying to do?"

Daisy grabs my arm and leans into me. Her eyes flit between her mum and dad.

Aunt Bev shoves a piece of bacon in my bread and pushes it in my hand. "Go on, both of you. It's time you went to school."

I take Daisy's hand and we run along the seafront. Instead of heading up the hill, I lead her along the coastal road.

Daisy grips my hand tightly in hers. "We're not going to school, are we?"

I shake my head. "We're going to see the dolphin."

The vet's car and Greg's pickup are among the few cars in the headland parking lot. I'm relieved to see no one else on the path above the pool. Carl is sitting outside one of the tents, wrapped in a sleeping bag. He waves for us to come on down. Felix and his dad are down there too.

Daisy and I slip under the police tape and clamber down the steps.

The rocks are deep purple in early morning shadow. The sea is pale blue. A thin mist hangs above the water. It's cool now, but it's going to be a hot day later; I can feel it. A notched dorsal fin slices through the water's surface beyond the tidal pool.

Carl looks at us and grins. "We've got good news. The mother dolphin did come back."

"We know." Daisy beams.

I nudge her in the ribs. "We always thought she would."

A mobile phone rings from inside the tent. "That's mine," says Carl. He crawls in the tent to answer it.

Felix's dad glances at his watch and frowns at us. "Shouldn't you both be on your way to school?"

"We just wanted to see the white dolphin," I say.

"Us too," says Felix. "We can give you a lift, can't we, Dad?"

Felix's dad nods. "Well, we'd better not be long. We'll be late as it is."

I turn to Daisy, but she's already walked away from us, across the rocks to the pool's edge.

"She's still mad at me, isn't she?" says Felix.

I smile. "She hasn't worn her fairy outfit since."

I follow Felix. He walks slowly across the uneven surface, holding onto boulders with his good arm to stop himself from falling on the rocks.

"Did you find anything on the memory stick?" I ask.

Felix shakes his head. "It's password locked. I've tried your name and *Moana*, and lots of others, but I haven't cracked it yet. Is there anything you can think of that your mum would use?"

I shrug my shoulders. It could be anything from her favorite food to the Latin name for starfish.

I duck under the white cover and crouch down next to Daisy. Beside me in a bucket are the remains of a dark brown liquid. Straggly pieces of entrails stick like cooked spaghetti on the bucket's sides. I wrinkle my nose. It stinks of fish. Greg is in the water supporting the flotation raft. In front of the dolphin stands a woman, holding up a funnel attached to a long tube that passes into the dolphin's mouth.

The woman smiles at me. "So you must be Kara. I've heard all about you from Carl. I'm Sam, the vet, by the way."

I smile back and look at the white dolphin. I lean forward, so I can look into her eye. She blinks and looks back at me. I wonder if she recognizes me, if she remembers who I am. "Will she get better now?" I ask.

Sam nods. "She's got a fighting chance. Once she can balance in the water and feed herself, we can set her free."

Daisy pushes back her curls of hair. "Can we help look after her?"

Sam laughs. "I don't think you'd like this job." She points to the thick brown liquid in the funnel. "It's dolphin baby food! Pureed fish and antibiotics!

When the swelling in her mouth goes down, we'll try her with whole fish."

Daisy takes her shoes and socks off and dangles her feet from the pool edge. "What's her name?"

Sam shrugs her shoulders and smiles. "She hasn't got a name."

"She has to have a name," says Daisy.

"I'm sure she has a dolphin name," says Sam. "Every dolphin has its own signature whistle, a name they call themselves."

"We have to find her a name," says Daisy. She slides knee-deep into the water and reaches out to stroke the dolphin.

Sam shakes her head. "We mustn't get her used to human contact. It's really hard, I know. But it's best for her."

I jump when a flurry of black wings rushes past me. A jackdaw tips the bucket and flaps off with a piece of fish tail in its mouth. I watch it fly up above the Blue Pool and see a figure walking slowly along the clifftop path.

"The Bird Lady," whispers Daisy.

Felix shades his eyes against the sun to look at her. "The Bird Lady? Who's she?"

I glare at Daisy and nudge her in the ribs. I don't want her to say anything about me going to see Miss Penluna.

"I know her," says Sam. "She sometimes brings sick birds to the clinic."

Daisy clings on to my sleeve. "She says dolphins are the angels of the seas."

Sam smiles. "Angels?" she says. "Yes, maybe they are."

The white dolphin glows pearly pink in the early morning light.

"Then that's what we'll call her," says Daisy, a big grin on her face. "We'll call her Angel."

25

"Angel?" asks Carl.

Daisy nods. "She's got to have a name."

Carl stares at his mobile phone in his hand. "That's just what the man said to me. He said she had to have a name."

"What man?" I ask.

Carl frowns and puts his phone in his back pocket. "A journalist from the local paper. There's been loads of interest in the dolphin, especially since we put her story on the Marine Life Rescue website," he says. "There are newspapers and TV and environmental groups who want to come and see her. I've got to find a venue for a press conference for Saturday. I've rung up the town hall, but they say no. They say it's too short notice."

"No surprise there," says Greg. "Dougie Evans is on the committee."

I fold my arms and lean back against the rocks. "We'll soon have coachloads of people coming here to our bay. Everyone will want to see her. She'll become like a sideshow in a theme park."

"People love to see dolphins," says Carl. "It gives us a chance to tell them about what the Marine Life Rescue team do, and the dangers facing our sea life, too."

Felix slaps the water with his hand. "But that's it!" he shouts. "That's exactly what we need her for. We need to use her to tell them about the reef."

I shake my head. "And make her something for people to stare at? People should be interested in the reef without putting a dolphin on display."

Felix rolls his eyes. "It's not the same, is it? I mean, what d'you think people want to read about, 'Save the Sea Squirt' or 'Save the Dolphin'?"

I scowl at him. "Okay, so how do you suggest we do it?"

"Use the Internet," says Felix. He's grinning from ear to ear. "Websites, social-networking sites, blogs, and Twitter; get people involved."

I shake my head. "It wouldn't work."

Felix throws his hand up. "*Why* not, Kara? I can't believe you don't want to give it a go. We could get an online petition for people to sign to stop the dredging of the reef."

"It's no use," I say. "You can put up all the stupid blogs you'd like. You can get a million people to sign the petition, but nothing will work. Nothing will work unless we can convince the trawler owners to save the reef."

I turn my back on Felix and flick small stones across the flat rocks.

"Come on," says Felix's dad. "It's time I got you all to school."

• • •

We sit in silence on the way to school. I hold my bag tightly against my chest and stare out of the car window. I can't believe Felix and Carl want to use Angel like some circus act for the newspapers and TV to come and gawp at.

By the time we've dropped Daisy off, we're late for lessons. I watch Felix walk along the corridor to his math class. His steps are short and jerky. It's all right for him; he could use it as an excuse for being late. I would if it were me. I know I'll be told off for being late again. It's almost the end of term. So instead of climbing the stairs, I walk out of the side door onto the playground and sink down against the thick trunk of the horse chestnut tree.

I curl up in the fork of tree roots, hidden from the school, and rest my head on my schoolbag. My eyes ache with lack of sleep and my thoughts spin out like threads of cloud across the blue, blue sky. The shade beneath this tree is cool and still. Somewhere above, a blackbird sings. A breeze sifts through the dense leaf cover and draws me into sleep.

"There you are," says Felix.

I open my eyes and sit up.

Felix is standing in front of me, frowning. "I've been looking everywhere for you."

I get up and brush grass and dirt from my skirt. "What time is it?"

"It's the end of break," he says and frowns. "Mrs. Carter wants to see us both."

I guess we're in trouble for being late this morning, but I've gone past caring. There's only two more days left. Two more days and I can forget all about school. I follow Felix along the corridor to Mrs. Carter's office. He knocks and pushes open the door. Inside the room, Chloe and Ella and several others from our year sit on cushioned chairs around the table. I glance at Mrs. Carter. I wonder what they're doing here as well.

"Come on in, Kara," she says. Her smile unnerves me.

Felix sits down next to Chloe.

Mrs. Carter points at a seat for me to sit down, but I don't take it. I stand beside the door. "Felix has been telling us about the dolphin you both helped to save."

I glance at Felix.

"We'd all like to offer our help too," she says.

Ella's smiling. Chloe is fiddling with her bracelet, but looks up at me through her bangs.

I don't want this to be happening. I can't believe Felix has been telling everyone at school.

"What do you think, Kara?" Mrs. Carter is still smiling at me, waiting.

"There are plenty of helpers at the moment," I say. "And it's a bit crowded down at the Blue Pool. No one's allowed to touch her, anyway."

I see Ella's face fall.

"Felix suggested a way maybe the whole school can be involved," Mrs. Carter says.

I shake my head. Angel's our dolphin. We found her. Now Felix wants everyone to have a piece of her too.

I take a couple of steps back to the door and glare at Felix. "Thank you, but we don't need any help."

Felix glares back at me. "You're wrong, Kara,"

he says. "If we want to save the reef, we need all the help we can get."

"We're fine just as we are," I say.

Mrs. Carter opens her arms wide. "Felix is right, Kara," she says, "We all want to protect the bay too. None of us want the dredging ban lifted. I've offered Carl the school hall for the conference he needs. There'll be everyone from the press and politicians to the trawlermen here. It's our chance to show everyone how much we all care about our bay."

"We're going to make posters and put them up all around the hall," says Chloe.

"Come on, Kara," pleads Ella. "It's important to us all."

Chloe nods. "It's our bay too, Kara."

I look around at them all. "D'you really think it could work?"

Felix pushes himself forward on his seat. "It has to work, Kara," he says. "The ban is lifted in less than one week's time. It's the only thing left that we can do."

26

I make sure I get to the school just after lunch on Saturday. I thought I'd be early, but I'm not the first one here.

I hold the main doors open for Greg. He's carrying a big cardboard box in his arms. I can see rolled-up posters and bits of dried seaweed sticking out of the top. "Back at school already, Kara?" he says with a grin. "On the first day of the holidays? You must be keen."

I laugh and follow him into the school hall. I wouldn't miss this for the world.

I can't believe how much we've managed to do in so little time. We stopped lessons for the last two days and did a school project on the reef instead. Our year made a huge mural of the coral reef along one side of the hall. Eighth graders made a timeline of our town with fishing boats and nets and shoals of tinfoil fish. Only Jake and Ethan didn't get involved. Jake didn't even come in to school at all on the last day.

"What d'you think?" asks Chloe.

She's pinning up the last photo on a display board just inside the doors. These are the first photos Carl took on the day we found her to new photos Chloe took today.

"It's great," I say. I stare into the photo Chloe took this morning of Angel swimming on her own in circles in the Blue Pool.

"She's eating by herself too," says Chloe.

I look at another photo, a close-up of Angel's

mouth. The deep wound has almost healed. Apart from a line of thick scar tissue that dips down at the corner of her dolphin smile, there's no sign that she's had an injury at all.

Felix's dad walks past with a stack of chairs. "Hey, Kara, can you give us a hand?"

Felix's mum is here too, putting chairs out in rows. The chairs almost fill the hall from front to back.

"How many d'you think will come?" I ask.

Felix's dad shrugs his shoulders. "We'll find out soon enough," he says.

Felix hands me small postcards with a photo of Angel on the front. "Can you help with these?"

I turn one over in my hand. "What are these for?" I ask.

"I made them yesterday," Felix says. "I thought we'd put them on all the seats. They're for people to sign on the other side and put in the petition box to stop the dredging."

I turn one over and see the black lettering on the

other side. "They're great, Felix," I say. "Really great."

Felix looks at me and grins. "I hoped you'd like them."

I walk up and down the rows putting cards on the chairs. At the back of the hall, Carl is setting up the laptop for the big screen up on the stage. It's less than two hours until the meeting and less than two days until the trawlers can dredge the reef.

More children and parents join us and help stick pictures on the wall and put a display of different shells and seaweeds on a table. When the last picture has gone up, Greg walks in from the kitchens with a tray of drinks.

I take a glass of orange soda and flop down next to Felix. "We're done," I say. "There's nothing more we can do now."

The doors open and swing shut, and Mrs. Carter walks through. She unrolls a long sheet of paper. "I've just come across this on the Internet," she says.

Ella helps to pin it to the board, then stands in front of it and reads the words out loud. "'To the dolphin alone, beyond all other, nature has granted what all good philosophers seek: friendship for no advantage.'"

Mrs. Carter nods. "Plutarch, an ancient Greek philosopher, wrote that two thousand years ago. It's important for today, too. Friendship for friendship's sake, and not because we think there's something else we can gain. It's amazing how dolphins have an effect on people."

"The Maoris in New Zealand believe dolphins carry the spirits of their ancestors," I say. I stop and look around. Everyone is quiet, listening.

Mrs. Carter smiles. "I wonder what the Maori name for dolphin is."

I stare into a picture of a dolphin above Mrs. Carter's head. I try to remember. I know Mum told me once. I remember the name sounds like dolphin breaths bursting above the water.

"What is it then?" asks Felix.

His question's so direct. I turn to look at him.

He leans forward and stares at me. "Well?"

"It's 'te . . . pu-whee,'" I say.

"Are you sure?"

"I think so."

"How d'you spell it?"

"I don't know," I say. "Does it matter?"

Felix runs his hand through his hair. He looks at me and then at the clock. "I've got to go," he says. "It's worth a try."

"What?" I ask.

"Tell you later."

He gets up and pulls his dad away.

"Carl's giving his talk in an hour," I call after him.

But Felix and his dad have gone. The doors of the hall swing and slam shut behind them.

I help Greg and Mrs. Carter clear away the cups and take them to the sink in the kitchens.

"Goodness, look out there," says Mrs. Carter.

I stand on tiptoe to look out of the high

windows. I can't believe my eyes. "We won't fit them all in," I say.

Greg shakes his head. "Some will have to stand."

The parking lot is already full of cars, and some are lined up along the road. A long queue of people curls around the playground.

"Does Carl know?" I ask.

"He's gone to get changed," says Greg. "I don't think he'll know what's hit him."

I look out along the row of people. There are lots of tourists in bright shorts and beach gear. But I see lots of people I know from the town, too.

"That's Mr. Cooke, our local politician," says Mrs. Carter.

"That's got to be good," I say. "Maybe he can pass a law to stop the dredging."

Greg frowns. "That's up to politicians up in London," he says. "Most of them wouldn't know a cod from a mackerel if one hit them in the face."

Then I see who Mr. Cooke is talking to. I see Dougie Evans. I see them smiling, sharing a joke. I don't want Mr. Cooke to be on Dougie's side. I remember what Felix said about not giving up without a fight. There're less than two days until the dredging ban is lifted. Less than two days before the trawlers can haul their chains across the reef. We might never get this chance again.

This is it.

It has to work.

This is our one big chance to save the bay.

27

I push my way through the crowd of people milling in the entrance and take a seat next to Dad and Daisy at the front. The room is packed. People are lined up along the the walls. I see a group of fishermen a few rows from the front. Dougie Evans is leaning back in his chair, arms folded across his chest, a smug smile on his face.

"Dougie met some of the trawler owners at the pub at lunchtime," whispers Dad. "He told them all to protest about the petition for the dredging ban, told them it's their livelihoods being taken away."

I turn round to look at the sea of faces in the room. "I bet loads here will sign the petition to protect the bay."

Dad shakes his head. "It will only be a voluntary ban for now. You know it won't mean a thing if the fishermen don't agree."

The room is hot despite the open doors and windows. The murmur of voices hushes as a journalist and cameraman walk up through the aisle and take a stand in a corner at the front. The local radio is here too, about to broadcast the meeting live.

"Where's Felix?" I whisper. "He should be here by now." I glance back over my shoulder at the crowded room. Maybe Felix can't push his way through. I get up to go and look, but Dad pulls me back down.

"Carl's about to talk," whispers Dad.

I watch Carl climb up the steps onto the stage and turn to face all the people.

Silence falls across the hall. Chair legs scuffle

and a baby cries somewhere at the back. I watch Carl. He looks so different in a suit and tie. His hair is brushed, and he wears thin gold-rimmed glasses. He shifts from foot to foot. He looks pale, too. I can hear the rustle of paper in his shaking hands.

I cross my fingers for him.

It doesn't start well. The microphone doesn't work, and he's so soft-spoken that I guess people halfway back can't hear him speak at all. Sunlight slants through the windows, and someone has to pull the curtains and switch the lights out to see the screen behind him. People listen when he shows pictures of Angel. There are gasps at the deep wounds in her mouth, and sighs at her taking her first fish.

But then Carl starts to talk about the bay and the project to save the coral reef. He shows graphs and pie charts on the screen, and talks about the different sorts of rock under the sea. He uses the Latin names of different sea animals and plants and holds up fragments of coral in his hand. I know the people at the back can't see. No one's really listening. All they want to hear about is Angel.

When Carl has finished speaking, the lights come on, and he asks for questions from the hall. Someone asks where they'll release the dolphin. Someone else asks if the white dolphin will change color. But no one is interested in the reef. It's out of sight, out of mind. Then Dougie Evans stands up. He walks up on the stage next to Carl, his cap in hand. He faces everyone, and I notice he's wearing his oldest clothes. They look worn and shabby.

"It's good to see so many here today," he says. "Tourists and locals, too."

His voice booms out across the hall. An easy smile sits on his face, but he doesn't fool me.

He opens his arms wide. "I hope you're all having a lovely time. But this lovely town of ours isn't just for sandcastles and holidays. We've been fishing from this port for hundreds of years. It's our livelihood. When tourists go home, we've still got to make a living."

Everyone is listening now. It's hard not to. There's something about Dougie Evans that holds people. I glance across the room and see Jake looking smug.

"There's plenty of reef around this coastline," Dougie goes on. "There's plenty for everyone. We dredge for scallops in our bay, like the farmers plow their fields."

The room is silent. I look around and see all eyes fixed on Dougie.

He puts his fist against his chest. "Fishing is the heart of this town!" he shouts out. "Always has been. So if you still want the freshest scallops on your plate, then support us too. Support the fishermen. Don't sign the petition for the ban."

The murmur of voices rises, and a ripple of applause flows back across the people. It's not just some of the fishermen who are clapping, but tourists, too. Dougie Evans takes a quick bow and steps down to take his seat again.

"Say something, Carl," I mutter under my breath.

But Carl just stands there, shuffling his feet while Dougie grins, victorious.

"STOP!"

Heads turn to the shout from the back of the hall. Dougie Evans squints to see who's calling. I turn too. Chairs scrape and feet shuffle as people clear a space for Felix to get through the aisle. He stops in front of me, the dolphin memory stick clutched in one hand. "Kara, I've found something, something important."

"What?" I say.

Voices are rising in the room. It's hot and stuffy. There's nothing to keep people here now. I see people at the back of the hall get up to leave.

Felix glances at them too. "You've got to buy me some time. Stop them from going. Get up on stage and say something, anything you want about the bay. Two minutes, that's all I need. Tell them they're about to see what they could lose."

I shake my head. "I can't."

Felix glares at me. "Just do it."

I watch him walk back down the aisle.

I've never stood in front of a crowd like this before. I don't know what Felix has found, but I can't lose this chance. I climb up the steps and face the audience. I don't even know what I'm going to say. The sea of faces stares back at me. I feel sick and dizzy. I see Jake's mouth curl in laughter. Dougie Evans is watching me too. His eyes bore right through me. I look around the walls of the hall, at the mural of traditional fishermen, fishing boats and nets and barrels of salted fish.

"Dougie Evans is right," I say. My voice comes out much louder than I expect. The hall is silent, listening. A few people sit back down in their chairs. "Fishing *is* the heart of this town." I look around. This is my one big chance. "Our small boat fished from this harbor a hundred years ago. Back then, she would have come home full of pilchard and herring, so full, the fish would be spilling over her sides back into the sea." I swallow hard. The back of my throat is dry, like sawdust. I look around and fix my eye on Dougie Evans. "But she can't do that anymore. We've taken all the fish from our seas. Dougie Evans's trawlers have to go farther and deeper to find fish, and even then they sometimes come back empty. Now we're dredging our bay for scallops, tearing up the reef. I wonder, will we still be fishing here at *all* in another hundred years?" I glance across the hall. There's no sign of Felix, but I remember what he wanted me to say. "You're about to see what we could lose."

I stand there in the silence and look around the hall. I don't know what's meant to happen now. I climb down the steps and sit next to Dad.

The hall lights go out.

The whole room holds its breath.

A clear voice cuts through the silence. I have to grab the edges of my seat. My head spins, and I feel myself tip forward.

I hear Mum speaking through the darkness.

28

"Let me take you on a journey through our last great wilderness, a place of mountains and deep valleys. Yet it doesn't lie in some distant land, but here, below the surface of our cold Atlantic sea."

Dad takes hold of my hand. The room is silent. The huge screen on the stage is dark at first. A faint greenish glow in the center of the screen becomes brighter and brighter, and we are rising up, toward the sun shining through the surface of the water.

Bright green kelp fronds reach upward to the rippling mirror screen of light. A seal swims up to the camera, his nose almost touching the lens. It's as if he's watching everyone in the hall. His big dog-eyes are chocolate brown. He snorts a breath. Silver bubbles spiral upward, and he twists away, flippers pressed together, his gray body sliding through the water. And we're twisting through the water too; down, down, down through shafts of rippling sunlight, past rocks jewelled with pink-and-green anemones, down past coral mounds and feather stars and sea fans.

This must have been the last film Mum made.

Her voice guides us into dark green waters full of rocks encrusted with soft, pink corals and yellow sponges. A cuckoo wrasse hovers in midwater, bright blue and yellow, lit by a flashlight. A purple sea slug threads its way through reddish seaweed. Beneath all this, the rocky bed is alive with corals and urchins. A velvet swimming crab scuttles by. Everything is alive in here.

But suddenly a tearing sound rips through the

hall. The image on the screen changes and fills with metal chains and billowing mud and sand. When the mud settles all that's left is a gravelly seabed, littered with broken sea fans. The silence in the hall is still and deep.

Mum's voice speaks out one last time.

"Unless we protect our oceans, there will be nothing left but wasteland. We are not farmers of the sea. We never sow, we only reap."

The lights come on. No one speaks. We've all been brought back from another world, the images still vivid in our minds. Mum's voice is still ringing in my head. Carl climbs back on the stage. He clutches his notes in his hand and is about to speak, but a ripple of applause starts at the back of the room and rolls forward like a wave. I look across to see some of the fishermen nodding. Others are just staring at the screen, transfixed. Only Dougie Evans is sitting, hands folded tight across his chest. Jake is glaring at me from across the room. I turn away. I don't want to spoil this moment. I heard Mum's voice again. I want to hold it deep inside. Hold it and keep it there forever.

"I'm sorry I couldn't warn you," says Felix. "I didn't have time."

I roll my jeans up and dip my feet into the pool. Angel glides past on her side, her small eye watching me. I stretch my leg out, and she lets my toes brush against her smooth, warm body.

"How did you find out?" I ask.

Felix sits beside me on the rocks and holds out the memory stick. *"Tepuhi,"* he says. "I should have thought of it before. The Maori name for dolphin. It's the password. The one your mum used for the memory stick."

I take it from him and curl my fingers around the molded plastic dolphin. It seems strange to think that it holds a memory of Mum, a snapshot of the past, as if it holds part of her inside it too. "Was there anything else on there?"

"Not much else," he mumbles.

I want to ask him what he means by "not much else," but Carl sits down beside us.

"I'm glad that's over," he says. His tie hangs loose around his neck, and his pressed trousers are now crumpled. He runs his hands through his hair. "I couldn't have done it without you."

"D'you think it'll make a difference?" I ask.

"There were loads of signatures for the voluntary ban on dredging," he says. "I counted hundreds of names."

"What about the fishermen?" I say.

"I don't know," Carl says. "I guess we'll find out soon enough."

Angel swims past us again and slaps the water with her tail. I reach out to run my hand along her head and the bumpy scar across her jaw.

Carl frowns. "She's becoming too dependent on us," he says, "and we're worried for her mother, too. There were lots of boats out on the bay today. She could get injured by their propellers." He stands up to wipe the water from his trousers, then crouches down beside me and Felix. "I shouldn't be telling you this, because no one else must know . . ."

I feel my heart sink, because I know just what he's going to say. "You're going to let her go, aren't you?"

Carl nods. "Sam thinks she's ready. But we don't want lots of people around when we release her."

Angel lifts her head above the water. It's as if she's listening to us too. I want her to go back into the wild, but I feel torn apart inside. I know that once she's gone, it could be the last time I see her.

"When?" I ask.

"Tomorrow," says Carl. "We release her on the beach, at dawn."

29

I'm the first on the beach. I wrap my arms around me and wish I'd brought my coat. The Milky Way is a river of stars across the sky. I remember Mum telling me the Maori story of *Tama-rereti* and how he scattered tiny pebbles into the sky to light up his way, and how the Sky God put *Tama-rereti*'s canoe up in the sky as the Milky Way to show how all the stars were made. I dig my toes into the cool sand and listen to the line of breaking surf. I want to see the mother dolphin. I strain my ears for the sound of a dolphin blowhole opening out on the water.

"Kara, is that you?"

I turn.

Dad is walking toward me, silhouetted against the street lights. "I heard you leave the house. What are you doing out here?"

"Carl's releasing Angel at dawn." I can't stop my teeth from chattering. A cool wind is blowing off the shore.

Dad takes off his fleece and slips it over me. The sleeves are far too long and the fleece comes down to just above my knees. Dad hugs me tight against him, and we watch the dawn spread across the eastern sky, a pale strip of light fading out the stars. A flock of sanderlings skims low across the beach and settles farther along the shoreline.

"Here's Carl," says Dad.

A pickup drives toward us, its headlights reflecting in the wet sand.

"I hope Felix and his dad get here in time," I say.

The pickup stops beside us, and Carl and Greg jump down, followed by Felix's dad and Sam. I lean over the back of the pickup to see Felix sitting by Angel's head. Angel is wrapped in wet towels on the yellow flotation raft.

Carl scans the water. "Any sign of the mother dolphin?"

I shake my head. "I hope she's not waiting by the pool."

I take a front corner of the raft with Dad, and we all help lift Angel down.

She's heavy, a solid mass of bone and muscle. I rest one hand on her head as we carry her to the water. Her breaths are short and shallow, her eyes wide open.

"Not too deep," says Carl. "Let's wait for her to get used to the water. We don't want her swimming off too early."

We float Angel out into the waves until we're waist deep in water. The waves are breaking farther out, running to the shoreline in steps of broken surf. Angel is strangely calm, as if she's waiting too. I feel her clicks and whistle pass right through me, invisible pulses of sound spreading out through the dark waters of the bay.

The sun's rim rises above the hills behind us, turning the sea to liquid gold.

I feel Angel's body tense. She's still and silent, listening.

Maybe I can feel the vibrations of whistles through the water too, because I sense her mother near us.

"Pfwhooosh!" She surfaces close by.

"Just watch her," says Carl. "She could turn aggressive if she wants her calf."

Angel flaps her tail, desperate to swim.

Carl and Greg deflate the two long cushions of the raft and let it slip beneath her. I run my hands along her back one last time as she surges forward to meet her mother. They swim side by side, their bodies touching, and slide together beneath the sea.

Two plumes of warm breath rise in the chill dawn air.

I watch the space where they had been and feel a strange emptiness deep inside.

It's not for what I've lost.

But for what I hope will be.

30

Carl offers us a lift home in the pickup truck. My shorts are soaking wet and I'm freezing cold. I sit in the back with Dad and Felix. We bump along the rippled sand and turn up the slipway to the coastal road. The newsagent is open early. The shopkeeper is already putting the papers on the display racks outside. Dad raps on the window for Carl to stop, and he jumps out to buy Aunt Bev some bread and a local paper.

I snatch the paper from his hands. On the front is a huge picture of Angel. I flick to the inside pages and see a double spread with photos of Carl and Dougie and the school hall. Daisy and I are pictured too.

"What does it say?" I ask. I push the paper into Felix's hand.

Felix holds up the paper. "'Save our Seas: Locals and tourists filled the school hall yesterday to give their support to the marine reserve . . .'"

Felix is silent for a moment while he skim-reads the article. He breaks out in a huge grin. "We've done it. Listen here . . . 'Local fishermen signed the petition for the voluntary ban on fishing and dredging the area, while a law to ensure the bay gets statutory protection is put through parliament. The petition was signed by more than six hundred people in less than two hours.'"

"So the fishermen are on our side," I say. "They promise not to dredge the bay until a new law is passed to protect the reef." I can't help grinning. I never dreamed it would happen like this. We've saved Angel and we've saved the bay.

"We've got to remember this moment," Felix says. "It doesn't get much better than this."

I nod, because he's right, and nothing can take away this feeling.

Nothing.

Not even Dougie Evans's jeep parked in Aunt Bev and Uncle Tom's drive.

Carl pulls up outside the house. We can hear raised voices coming through the open kitchen window. Uncle Tom and Dougie Evans are doing the shouting. Aunt Bev is standing with her back to us, pressed against the kitchen sink.

"Do you want us to come in with you?" asks Felix's dad.

Dad shakes his head and looks grim. "It's okay," he says. "I guess Dougie Evans has seen the paper too."

Dad and I jump down from the pickup. I wave

at Felix as they turn the corner and disappear out of sight.

I follow Dad up the path toward the door. I try hard not to step on the cracks in the paving stones, but Dougie Evans flings the door open and stops in front of us. I see he has the same paper in his hand.

He chucks it on the ground. "Means nothing, this," he snarls. "It's not worth the paper it's written on." He kicks it with his foot, and the pages scatter into the air.

Dad stands back to let him through, and he glares at me as he passes. I think he'll walk right past, but he stops and turns back to face me.

"Saving bloody dolphins like your mum, eh?" His face is pressed close up to mine. Sweat glistens on his forehead. "Look what happened to her."

"Go home, Dougie." Dad pushes himself in front of me. "Just go home." Dad's voice is calm, but his hands are clenched.

I try to slip in front of Dad. I want him to be safe, but Dad just holds me back.

"No one tells me what to do!" Dougie shouts. "No one."

He turns away and storms down the path to his car. He spits on the pavement, climbs in, and roars away.

And we are left in dust and silence.

Dad puts his arms around me. "Ignore it," he says.

I lean into Dad and walk into the house with him. But I can't help thinking Dougie Evans would rip up the whole sea and everything in it if he could.

Aunt Bev is standing at the sink, her hand across her belly. Uncle Tom goes to put his arm around her, but she shrugs him off. "You didn't listen to me, did you?"

Uncle Tom sits down at the table and puts his head in his hands.

"What happened?" Dad asks.

Aunt Bev shakes her head and stares at her husband. "I told him not to sign that petition, but he wouldn't listen."

Dad looks between them. "Bev, what happened?"

"He's lost his job. Dougie fired him just now."

Dad pulls up a chair next to Uncle Tom. "He can't just do that," he says.

"Of course he can," snaps Aunt Bev. "He's Dougie Evans. He does what he likes. You should've known that, Tom."

Uncle Tom gets up. He grabs his jacket and walks to the door.

"Where are you going now?" snaps Aunt Bev.

"Out," he says. "I need fresh air."

He pushes past us, and I hear the front door slam shut.

"We need the money, Tom," she calls after him through the open window. "What are we going to do without money?"

I back away to the door too. Aunt Bev's in no fine mood. I expect the shouting to start at me and Dad, but she sinks into a chair. She pushes back thin strands of hair from her face and stares up at the ceiling.

"What am I going to do, Jim?" she says. "We've got no money for the rent this month."

Dad takes Aunt Bev's hand in his. "Things will work out, Bev. You'll see."

But Aunt Bev shakes her head. She doesn't even wipe away the tears that fall and soak dark drops onto the T-shirt stretched across her bulging belly.

"We can't keep you and Kara too," she says. "God knows how we'll keep ourselves."

Dad nods and sits with her, still holding her hand. "You've been good to us, Bev," he says. "I'm sorry."

I back out of the door and turn to head up the stairs. But Daisy's sitting on the bottom stair, Teddy-Cat clutched to her chest. Her face is puffy, and her eyes are red with tears.

"I don't want you to go," she says. She wraps her arms around me.

I hug her tight. "Come on, Daisy," I say. I put my arm round her, and we climb the stairs up to her bedroom. I sit next to her on the bed and hug her into me. "Carl released Angel this morning," I say.

"I wish I could have come," she says.

I stroke her hair. I feel bad that I didn't take her. But I couldn't have asked Aunt Bev. She'd never have let me go either. "She found her mother. She was waiting for her in the bay."

Daisy smiles and picks at the fluff balls on Teddy-Cat's fur.

"We saved the reef, too," I say. "There's a picture of you and me in the paper. We're famous, Daisy."

Daisy frowns. "Dougie Evans is mad at that."

"I know," I say. I can't help smiling. "But we've got the other fishermen on our side. They're not going to dredge the reef."

Daisy shakes her head. "Dad said he wouldn't do it. That's why Dougie Evans started shouting," says Daisy.

"Uncle Tom said *he wouldn't do* what?"

Daisy looks at me. Her bottom lip trembles. "I heard them in the kitchen, and Dougie Evans is going to do it anyway."

I feel my heart pump in my ears. I search her face. "Do what?" I ask.

Daisy hugs Teddy-Cat tight into her chest. "Dougie Evans said he's going fishing on the midnight tide. He's going to rip out every coral in the bay."

31

"It didn't make any difference, did it?" I say.

I turn the brittle skeleton of the pink sea fan over and over in my hand. A small piece comes away and falls onto the wet sand. Every day, more sea fans and corals are washed up on the shoreline. It's been nearly a month since the local fishermen signed the voluntary ban. But since then, more and more trawlers from other fishing towns up and down the coast have come to dredge the bay. It seems they don't care about the ban or the bay.

Felix flings a pebble into the waves. "Dad heard the local fishermen complaining, because they're not getting as many lobsters and crabs in their traps. And the fish market in town won't buy the scallops," he says. "At least they still support the voluntary ban. The trawlers that come here have to take their catch elsewhere."

I shake my head. "For now," I say. I know Uncle Tom managed to get work on another boat. He'll be out there soon too. And he's not the only local fisherman to go out on the trawlers. Dad heard them say it wasn't fair that other fishermen were taking their share of shellfish instead. I stare out to sea. At least it's been too rough to work these past few days. The high waves have washed up broken reef. I don't want to imagine what it looks like now. It must look like a ghost reef, like the pictures of torn-down rainforests, only under water, out of sight.

Felix pulls his hood up over his head. We're the only ones on the beach today. The clouds are low and heavy. They scud across the headland and the hills behind. Cold rain blasts in from the sea, horizontal.

"We saved Angel, though," says Felix. "It counts for something."

"I know," I say. "I wish we could see her again."

We've looked for the dolphins every day, but we haven't seen them since Angel was released. Carl asked us to record any sightings of dolphins or whales. He took us out one day in the Marine Life Rescue boat, and we saw basking sharks, their sail-like black dorsal fins cruising through the water and their huge white mouths gaping open, filtering plankton from the sea. We saw grey seals, too, their fish-fattened bodies stretched out on warm rocks, sleeping in the sun.

"I don't reckon we'll see much out there today," says Felix. "Come on. Let's get some food in town."

I stand up and wipe the sand from my hands. "Don't you ever stop eating?"

Felix grins. "Lunch was two hours ago. I'm starving."

We walk through the streets in town, but the

cafés are packed. Through the mist of condensation on the windows, I see families crowded around tables. Bags, coats, and umbrellas lie scattered around chairs.

"We could get some chips from the take-away and eat them in *Moana* under the cover," I say. "There's not much room, but we'd be dry."

"It'll do for now." Felix grins. "We'll have more room when I get my yacht for my solo trip around the world."

I laugh. "So you're still up for the regatta race next week?"

"Yep," he says. "Dad and I got around Gull Rock and back in under an hour and thirty minutes last time."

"Not bad," I say. But secretly I'm impressed. The fastest time Dad and I raced *Moana* was in one hour and forty-five, but I'm not telling Felix that. He and his dad have been out sailing nearly every day. I've watched them from the shore. I've watched, wanting to be out there too with Dad in *Moana*, like it used to be. But now, even on his days off work, he finds something else to do. He's just not interested anymore. It's as if he's turned his back on her. Maybe it's because he can't face losing her. Maybe that's the way he feels about me.

Felix and I take our chips from the counter. I slip mine inside my coat to keep them dry, and we turn down Rope Walk, a quicker way to the harbor. Rain hammers on the rooftops and water pours out of gutters and across our path. The cobbles shine wet, the moss between them damp and slippery. Felix picks his way slowly down, but I hurry ahead, keen to get out of the rain. I hear him shout. I turn and see him stumble to the ground, and his knees hit the hard stone cobbles. His chips scatter into the rivulets of water.

I run back and kneel down beside him. "Sorry, I shouldn't have rushed on."

I offer my hand to help him up, but he pushes me away and swears under his breath. I try to scoop up some of his chips, but even the ones still in the packet have turned to mush. The seagulls are pacing up and down behind us, ready for an easy meal.

Felix pushes himself up and thumps his hand against the wall. "I *hate* being like this sometimes."

His jeans are ripped at the knees. Dark red bloodstains spread across the frayed denim.

He leans against the wall and kicks the chip packet toward the seagulls. "Out on the water, I can do anything anyone else can do. It's like my boat is part of me." He thumps the wall again. "Out there, I'm free."

I nod, because I know just what he means. *Moana* feels part of me. She keeps us safe, a protective shell around Mum and Dad and me.

The wind gusts up from the harbor walls and whips my hair across my face. I wrap my coat tightly around me and feel my packet of chips burn warm against my skin. The smell of vinegar and salty chips wafts up around my collar. "Come on," I say. "I've got loads in here. You can share mine." I'm starving too, and can't wait to eat them under *Moana*'s cover spread across the boom.

The harbor walls are empty. A few gulls march along the wall beside the waste bins, hoping for scraps of food. I look down along the line of pleasure yachts to see *Moana*. But her cover's been drawn back and there are two people sitting inside. Even from here I can see who they are. It's Ethan and Jake Evans.

I leave Felix on the harbor wall and climb down the ladder set into the granite blocks. I run along the dock, my feet thudding on the boards.

I stare at them in the boat. Crisp packets and a drink can lie scattered inside. "Get out!" I yell.

Jake and Ethan exchange glances. Ethan puts his feet up on the seats.

I climb inside *Moana*. "Get out of my boat."

Jake leans forward and smirks at me. "I think you'll find she's not your boat."

I scowl at him. "What d'you mean?"

Jake just smiles. "Take a look."

I look around *Moana*. Everything's the same. I open up the cubby under the foredeck. The flares and toolbox are still there, but our blankets have gone, and so have Dad's fishing tackle and the red tin cups.

I look up at Jake and he's still grinning. "Didn't your dad tell you? My dad bought her last weekend." He looks at the chip packet sticking out of the top

of my coat. "Your dad was in a hurry to sell her. Cheap as chips, she was."

I just stare at him. It can't be true.

But Jake's mouth forms in a thin, hard line. He holds up the keys to the locker under the foredeck. "So I think it's for me to say, get out of *my* boat."

I back out of *Moana* and climb the ladder. I shove the chips in Felix's hand. "I've got to go," I say. I run all the way to Aunt Bev's house and don't stop until I burst through the door. Aunt Bev's ironing shirts, watching the TV.

I stand in front of her. "Where's Dad?" I ask.

Aunt Bev tries to look around me. "He went out."

I switch the TV off. "Where?" I say.

She upends the iron and puts her hand on her hip. "What's this about, Kara?"

"He's sold her, hasn't he?" I try to blink back the tears. "He's sold *Moana*."

Aunt Bev stoops to pull the plug of the iron from the wall. "Sit down, Kara."

I don't sit down. "He's sold *Moana* to Dougie Evans."

Aunt Bev reaches out to touch my arm, but I step away. "He said he couldn't bring himself to tell you."

I just stare at her in blank silence.

"Don't be angry at him, Kara. He's trying to get his life back. God knows, he needs to."

"Where is he?" I ask.

Aunt Bev fiddles with a button on a shirt. "He's gone to Exeter for the day."

"Exeter!" Dad didn't mention this to me. "Why Exeter?"

Aunt Bev takes a deep breath. I watch her fold the shirt, running long straight creases down the sleeves and seams. She lets her breath out slowly and lays the shirt on the pile next to her.

"I shouldn't be telling you this," she says. She smooths the front of the shirt and straightens the collar. "But he's gone for a job interview. Don't ask what. He wouldn't even tell me. But he told me he was doing this for you."

I storm past her out of the room. She calls after me, but I run up the stairs to Daisy's bedroom, glad she's out at Lauren's today.

I curl up under my duvet and lie in empty silence.

I can't believe we've lost her.

Moana isn't ours.

That shell around Mum and Dad and me has broken.

It feels as if nothing can protect us anymore.

32

I sit with Felix on the wooden boards of the merry-go-round in the park. Rainwater soaks through my jeans, and the cold metal of the bars of the merry-go-around burn into my skin. It feels like a winter storm, although it's summer, still. The skies are low and heavy, and the sea is a shifting mass of gray and green. All the fishing boats have run for home, all except Dougie Evans's. His trawlers are still out there on the high seas.

It's been a week now since I found out Dad sold

Moana. I can hardly bring myself to speak to him. It's not as if he speaks to me these days, anyway. I've lost Mum and now I've lost *Moana*. It feels as if I'm losing Dad now too. He hasn't even mentioned his trip to Exeter, and I'm not going to ask him. It's not as if I can do anything. The baby's due any day, and Dad and I will have to find somewhere else to live.

I push the merry-go-round round with my feet. "Are you still sailing in the regatta race tomorrow?"

"If it's not canceled," says Felix. His hood is pulled over his head, and the storm collar of his coat is drawn across the lower half of his face, so only his eyes are showing.

"I hope you win," I say. "You deserve to."

He pushes back his hood. "I asked Dad if you could sail with me tomorrow instead of him, but he says I'm not ready yet."

"Thanks." I smile. "But I reckon your dad wants to do this with you too."

I push faster with my feet, and the hills and sea spin all around us.

"You know that sailing coach Dad got for me?" says Felix.

I nod. "I saw you with him out on the water."

Felix holds on to the merry-go-round with his good arm and leans out over the spinning concrete. "He wants to put me in the junior training squad for the Paralympics sailing team."

I slam my foot down. The merry-go-round scrapes to a halt. "You're kidding! Why didn't you tell me before? That's fantastic, Felix. Brilliant." I mean it, too.

He pulls the storm collar from his face and looks right at me. "One of the race categories is for a disabled and an able-bodied sailor. Would you do it with me?"

The question takes me by surprise. I've never sailed any other boat except *Moana*.

"We'd make a great team," he says. "We wouldn't argue . . . much." He's grinning now. "And we'd do all our training here, in the bay. We'll train in my boat."

I stare at the ground. I'd love the chance to sail

again, especially to race with Felix, but for all I know, Dad's got a job in Exeter. Soon we'll be far away from here. I shake my head. "I don't know, Felix," I say. "I don't think it would work."

"But, Kara . . ."

"Just leave it," I snap. I stand up and walk away from him to the park fence. The town is sprawled out beneath me. The houses are darkened by the rain, and the harbor is full of boats sheltering from the storm.

In the distance I see Dougie Evans's trawlers rear up on the horizon. Maybe it would be better to be far away from here. I don't think I could bear to see Dougie Evans sailing *Moana* in the bay. Felix leans on the fence next to me, and we watch the trawlers come back across the heaving sea, like wolves returning from their hunt. Their prows rise over waves and slice down, sending up plumes of spray. A flock of seagulls trails in their wake, bright against the slate-gray sky. I guess the trawlers have come back with full nets this time.

"I'm sorry I snapped," I say.

"Just think about it," says Felix. "Promise me?"

I nod and stuff my hands deep in my pockets. "I'd better go. Aunt Bev wants me back for lunch."

I walk with Felix across the playground. The wind whistles through the top bars of the jungle gym, like a gale through a mast. Big puddles spread across the pavement and rain shines off the seesaw and the swings. Outside the gate we almost bump into Adam and his brother, Joe, running down the road, their footsteps slapping on the wet pavement.

Adam stops in front of us, his hands on his knees, panting. "Have you seen it?"

"What?" I say.

"The great white shark," says Adam. "Dad's heard that Dougie Evans has caught a great white shark in his nets."

I shake my head. Joe pulls Adam's arm, and they set off toward the harbor. I can't believe Dougie Evans has caught a great white shark. We don't get them in these waters. He's probably caught a basking shark. I know they can get to forty feet in length. But there's a doubt in my mind, because we sometimes get leatherback turtles washed up here from more tropical seas.

"Shall we take a look?" I ask Felix.

Felix shrugs his shoulders. "Can you face seeing Jake again?"

"It won't be for long," I say. "I bet loads of other people are down there too."

By the time Felix and I reach the harbor, a small crowd has gathered on the quayside beside one of Dougie Evans's trawlers. We walk past the fish market. I glance through the clear plastic flaps of the entrance into the cool, bright space inside. Yellow crates, full of fish, lie in rows along the concrete floor. Two of the fishermen inside are grinning widely. It's been a good trip for Dougie Evans and his men.

I look around for Felix, but Jake is suddenly beside me. "Hey, Kara," he says. "Ever seen a great white shark before?" He looks smug, but there's something else, something more than boasting in his voice.

I look beyond him to the crowd of people.

I can see something lying on the ground, half hidden behind rows of legs.

I try to push my way through, but Chloe's suddenly next to me, pulling me away.

I can hear Jake's voice again. "Come and see what my dad's caught in his nets."

Chloe pulls me harder. "Don't look," she says. Her eyes are red with tears. "Come away, Kara."

And suddenly I don't want to be here, because I know it's not a great white shark that Jake Evans wants me to see.

I want to turn away, but I can't. I catch glimpses of it, smooth and gray between the legs of people crowded round.

I see Felix on the far side of the crowd. He looks sick and pale.

Overhead, a gull screams.

I push my way through, following Jake. There is no great white shark or basking shark. On the bloodied concrete lies the still gray body of a dolphin. Its eye looks unseeing into the leaden sky. I follow the smooth curve of its back to the dorsal fin, to a deep notch at the base.

I fall forward on my knees and taste the sharp acid of bile in my mouth.

Angel's mother is dead.

33

I run. I don't stop running until I reach the cove and sink down in the soft, white sand. Thin trails of bright blood trickle down my arms into the water. I didn't feel the gorse and brambles cut my skin, I just had to get here. I had to get away. I lie down and let the water swirl around me, soaking through my jeans. I rest my head upon the sand and close my eyes. And it floods over me again, that she is dead. Her staring eye and broken face stay fixed inside my mind, and I can't wash them out, however hard I try. It feels like part of me has gone, as if the part that kept Mum close has gone now too.

I press my forehead on the wet sand and dig my fingers in. I want to push my way into the sand and let it cover me and lie here forever. It's sheltered here. The running furl of surf and the soft patter of rain are the only sounds.

I lie like this and let the water swirl up around my jeans and shirt, scouring a small trench of sand around me. A small, white pebble washes up the beach past my fingers. I watch the flecks of crystal catch the light. I turn to face the sea and watch it roll back down into the sheen of rain-spattered water, my cheek pressed into the sand. The waves rise and fall, like folds of gray-green silk.

"Pfwhooosh!"

I sit up.

I hear it again, that burst of dolphin breath. Angel is here, her white dorsal fin curving through the water. She's come back here to find her mother,

back to this cove where I first found her. But her mother isn't here this time. Just me.

I wade out into the water. It rises over my waist and chest, and I can feel it pull on the heavy material of my jeans. I can see her again, not far from me. Her eye is a pale pinkish-gray. Her skin is the color of pearl. She sends a series of whistles and clicks, and I sense she's calling to her mother. I reach out to touch her, but she slides away and disappears underwater. I wade farther out. The waves swell under me and lift me up, out of my depth.

"KARA!"

I turn to see Felix and his dad standing at the clifftop.

"Kara, get out of there!" Felix's dad yells. He's waving both his arms at me.

Felix starts to slide forward on the ledge of dark gray rock. I know he won't be able to balance or find a safe way down. I turn and wade out of the water and up the beach, my feet heavy in the soft sand. I look once behind me. The cove is empty. Angel has gone.

When I reach the clifftop, Felix's dad pulls me up and wraps his coat around me. I feel cold. A deep, deep cold right through my bones. My hands are blue, and my fingers are blanched white.

"We've got to get you back, Kara," he says.

I look back down into the cove. "We can't leave her. She needs us now. We're all she's got."

"I've got to get you home," says Felix's dad. "Your dad's worried sick. He's out there looking too."

Felix's dad guides me to the road beyond a field gate. I can hardly put one foot in front of the other, and I can see Felix is struggling with the deep mud.

"Wait here, both of you," Felix's dad says. "I'll get the car and pick you up."

I slide down against the stone wall, out of the cold blast of wind, and watch Felix's dad jog away from us along the road. I press my back into the long grasses and fold my arms around my knees.

Felix slides down beside me and pulls his hood over his head. "People in town are mad at Dougie Evans for what he's done."

"Won't change anything," I say. I pull a piece of grass and wrap it around and around my hand. Dad was right. If we can't get all the fishermen on our side, then we can't save the reef. I don't think there's anything anyone can say or do to make someone like Dougie Evans change his mind. I wonder just how much he has to lose before he sees there will be nothing left.

I strip the wet seed heads from the grasses and flick them in the air. Mr. Andersen's car headlights find us through the drizzle.

Felix pushes himself to his feet and reaches deep into his pocket. "I'm not sure I should show you this," he says. He looks around at his dad's car bumping along the track. "I told Dad I wouldn't. But I thought if I were you I'd want to know."

"What?" I say.

Felix pulls out a white envelope and holds it in his hand. "There was something else on that memory stick," he says. "Dad looked into it. He's got some contacts."

"What, Felix?"

Felix stands in front of me and stuffs the envelope in my hand. "Hide it. Don't let my dad see."

I feel my heart thud against my chest. "Why didn't you tell me this before?"

"It might help you understand, that's all."

The car pulls up beside us and Felix's dad gets out. "Come on then, you two."

I slip the envelope under my sweater and slide in the backseat next to Felix. "Understand what?" I whisper.

Felix's dad twists round in his seat. "What are you two talking about?" he asks.

"Nothing," says Felix. He frowns and turns away.

We sit in silence as we bump along the rutted road. I hold the envelope tight against my chest and feel the corners press deep into my skin.

It holds something to do with Mum.

A missing key to where she is, maybe.

34

I stare at the photograph for the hundredth time. The shock of seeing Mum jolts through me once again. She's crouched down beside her diving gear, her hair tucked back behind her ears, a look of deep concentration on her face. I've seen her check her diving gear before, running through the list of safety checks in her head. It's pointless trying to talk to her like this. She can block out the outside world, absorbed in every detail of her work. Palm trees line the backdrop of a foreign port. The stern of a container ship fills the left half of the view and the right half shows a busy port with ships and cranes along docksides stretching into the distance. Rucksacks and boxes are piled up by Mum. I see her rucksack with them too. Shadows slant deep and long, so it must be early morning or late at night, I can't tell. I can almost imagine her face turn to look at me.

"Kara!"

I stuff the photo back under my pillow, where I slept on it all night. I don't want anyone to know. I've stayed in Daisy's bedroom all morning, hiding from Aunt Bev. She's been cleaning the house like mad, clearing out the cupboards and changing all the sheets.

"Kara!" Aunt Bev shouts again. "Felix's here. He wants to know if you're going to the regatta."

I climb down the stairs and into the kitchen. I can hear cartoons blaring from the sitting room and guess Daisy's trying to avoid her mum too.

Aunt Bev is leaning on her mop, beads of sweat pricked on her forehead. All the surfaces are cleared away and tidy, and I noticed the oven's sparkling clean. Even the windows have had a polish.

I tiptoe across the floor to Felix standing on the doormat and pull him into the hallway. "I didn't think you were going to the regatta," I say. "Didn't you hear the race is canceled? There's a storm coming."

Felix shrugs his shoulders. "I know, but I thought I'd see what was happening in town. Want to come?"

I nod. "I'll get my shoes."

I pull my sandals from the shoe rack in the hall. "I'm going into town with Felix!" I yell.

Aunt Bev leans against the doorframe and watches me strap up my shoes. She stretches and rubs the small of her back. "Take Daisy with you, Kara. I've too much to do today." She pulls some money from the tin above the microwave. "Here's ten pounds, to get a hot dog each."

I stuff the money into my pocket and walk with Felix along the coastal road. Daisy runs ahead of us, scattering gulls up into the sky.

"Did you look at it?" asks Felix.

I nod.

"It was taken at Honiara," he says, "a port on the Solomon Islands of Guadancanal. It was taken just before sunset on the night your mother disappeared."

We walk in silence for a while. I'm glad Felix's told me the facts, just plain and simple.

"How did you get it?" I ask.

"There was a folder on the memory stick marked 'Honiara.' There were lists of addresses: hotels, car rentals, and diving centers. A colleague of Dad's who's done some business out there made a few inquiries for him. He found this photo in the archives of a local paper."

I stop and turn to Felix. "So why haven't we seen this before, from the investigation at the time?"

Felix shrugs his shoulders. "Dad's colleague says the story wasn't run. It was bad publicity. Bad for tourism."

I lean on the railings and stare out to sea. The photo's proof that Mum went out diving that last night, but it doesn't tell what happened. There's no clue to where or why she went.

Despite the warm and humid air, the beach is empty. The sea is a pale, pearly green. A deep ocean swell lifts its polished surface into smooth ripples, like antique glass. Yet no one is in the water. It is calm, too calm. Everything is still. The flag above the chandlery hangs limp and loose. Even the seagulls have left the air and are lined up on roofs and chimney pots and along the sea wall. It feels as if the whole sky is pressing down on us. The storm's eye is above us now. This is the calm before the storm, and we are given time to think and breathe. Yet we are being watched it seems.

Daisy runs back and pulls my arm. "Come on," she says. "Let's go into town."

We walk through the narrow streets, under bunting hung between the shops and houses. Dad is outside the Merry Mermaid clearing plates. He waves and smiles to us as we pass, and I give a small wave back. In the square outside the town hall are several stalls and games. The mayor is in the stocks waiting for wet sponges. There's a coconut shy and a strongman game. A brass band is playing too, and a team of majorettes are twirling batons and marching up and down. I buy hot dogs and sit with Felix and Daisy on one of the benches in the square. I look across at Felix. I don't feel in the mood for this, and I can tell he feels the same way too. I let Daisy have the change from the money for the hot dogs and watch her run off to play a game of hook the duck and spend her money on the stalls.

It's only when she's run out of money that she comes back and flops beside us, a fluffy duck and a packet of fudge in her hands.

"Let's get you home," I say.

We walk toward the seafront along the road above the harbor. A small breeze lifts the edges of my shirt.

"Feel that?" I say.

Felix nods.

I look across to the flag above the chandlery. Its edges curl and ripple in the breeze. A new wind is blowing from the west. Dark clouds unfurl across the milk-white sky. A shiver runs down my spine and goose pimples prickle along my arms and legs, because out across the ocean a storm is coming, and we lie directly in its path.

We turn down a narrow stepped street between old cottages to the harbor.

"Hey, Two Planks!"

I glance behind. It's Jake and Ethan coming down the steps behind us.

Daisy takes hold of my hand and holds it tight.

"Hey, Kara!" shouts Jake. "Did you hear I'm moving?"

We keep walking, but Jake and Ethan catch up to us. Felix is struggling with the steps. The handrail stops halfway down the slope.

"Dad's buying one of them posh houses up on the hill that look over the bay," says Jake. "Massive garden. He said he'd get me a four-wheeler dirt bike, too."

I ignore Jake.

"Dad says he'll call it Shell House," says Jake. "Know why, don't you? It's from the profits of the scallops from the bay."

I want to keep walking, but Felix is at the top of a run of steps. I know he doesn't want me to help him, so I wait beside him while he makes his own way slowly down. His face is lined with concentration trying to balance on the steps.

"Shame the regatta's canceled," says Jake. "It's just I thought you'd like to see me sail *Moana* in the race."

"You can't even sail," I say.

"Ethan and me have sailed before." Jake laughs. "It's not that hard."

"You've done a couple weeks' dinghy sailing with school," I say. "That's all."

"Can't be that hard if he can do it." Jake jerks his head in Felix's direction. "He can hardly walk."

Ethan explodes with laughter.

I feel Felix tense up beside me.

"We'll race you anyway," says Jake, "us in *Moana* and you two in the loser boat. We'll even give you a head start."

I turn to face Jake. "There's no regatta today," I say. "Because there's a *storm* coming."

Jake throws his head back and laughs. "As if I'm scared of that!"

I turn away. It's not worth arguing anymore.

Jake strides off. "Come on, Ethan. Fancy a sail around Gull Rock?"

I watch them disappear around the corner of the end house on the street.

"They wouldn't," I say. "Would they?"

As we reach the harbor, big drops of rain slide from the sky and hit the pavement, spotting the pale cement dark gray. I feel the heavy drops land in my hair and on my clothes. The sky is almost black, and beyond the harbor, the sea heaves in big green swells. There are no white horses out there yet, just the rolling curves of waves.

"I don't believe it." I point down to the dock.

Jake and Ethan are in *Moana*. They've pulled back the tarpaulin from her boom, and I can see them rigging up the mainsail.

"They're crazy," says Felix.

"Dougie Evans would have a fit if he knew Jake was going out to sea," I say. "Come on, we have to stop them. Not just for their sake, but *Moana*'s. They'll wreck her if they try."

I climb down the ladder while Daisy follows Felix down the ramp. By the time I reach *Moana*, Jake and Ethan have the mainsail and the jib up. They've not even reefed the sails. A gust of wind catches the sail and swings the boom out over the water.

"Don't be stupid, Jake!" I yell.

But Jake just laughs and holds his hand out to feel the wind. "A summer breeze, that's all," he says.

But there's something more than bragging in Jake's eyes. There's fear too, as if he's gone too far and can't find his way back.

I pull *Moana* closer and her fenders bump against the dock.

"Don't do it, Jake," I say. "Your dad's lost Aaron. He doesn't want to lose you too."

Jake just stares at me. Heavy drops of rain slide from the sky and pit the water's surface. The drops fall faster, thick and heavy, and soon there is a screen of rain between us. I can't make out his face anymore. He unties *Moana* and pushes off with a paddle. Ethan's at the tiller. *Moana* slides across the water and thumps into a small cruiser moored against the other dock. Jake pushes off again, and this time Ethan points *Moana*'s bow to the harbor opening. She scrapes against the harbor wall, and I hear the scars tear in her side. Jake looks back once before *Moana* slips out of the harbor, the tip of her mast showing above the harbor wall. And it's only now I realize, too, that Jake and Ethan have no life jackets at all.

"We've got to stop them," I say. I look around the harbor, but the walls are empty. The rain has driven everyone away.

"We'll take my boat," says Felix. He leans down and starts untying the cover.

"Don't go," says Daisy.

I look at her. She's freezing cold and wet through. I kneel down beside her and hold her hands in mine. "Be brave, Daisy. Go and find my dad. He's in the Merry Mermaid. Tell him what's happened. Tell him to call the coast guard."

"Please don't go, Kara," she begs. Her eyes are big and full of tears.

"I have to," I say.

"You'll disappear. You won't come back."

I put my arms around her and wonder if this is how Mum felt when she left. "I'll be careful," I say. "I'll come back, I promise you."

Daisy pulls away from me. "I'm coming with you."

"You can't, Daisy," I plead. "It's too dangerous for you."

Felix looks up from what he's doing. "Daisy," he says, "someone has to call the coast guard. We might need help out there."

Daisy looks at him, and I see her bottom lip tremble.

"Right now, I need that fairy godmother, Daisy . . . ," says Felix, "she might be the one to save us."

A flicker of a smile crosses Daisy's face. She nods and wipes the tears from her face. "I'll go."

I watch her run along the dock. I shouldn't let her out of my sight, I know. What if she falls in the water or gets knocked down crossing a road? I try to push the thoughts from my mind and help Felix into his boat.

Felix starts pulling up the mainsail. "Put a life jacket on!" he yells. "I've got two here."

"Hang on!" I yell. I run down the dock, clamber into one of the sightseeing boats, and lift up one of the bench seats. I pull out two more life jackets, one for Jake and one for Ethan, and run back to Felix. We have to stop them before they get beyond the protection of the headland. Maybe we can make them turn round. I pull my life jacket on, climb in, and help Felix with his.

"Let's go!" shouts Felix.

I cast off and push the dinghy away. Felix guides us through the narrow gap between the harbor walls, out into the open sea, and out into the gray-green ocean swell.

The swell rolls in and slumps against the harbor walls. I can feel the power of the waves in the recoil that jars against the dinghy's hull. Jake and Ethan have put a lot of distance between us. *Moana*'s sails are full, and she is leaning heavily across the water.

Felix has put a reef in our sails, but she heels over and I sit out to balance her. I'm glad for the long centerboard in his boat and know at least we have less chance of capsizing. I glance at Felix, but his face is tightened in a knot of concentration. The headland is veiled in a sweeping curtain of rain. Gull Rock lies out at sea, pale gray against a darker sky. Beyond the headland the water is flecked with white horses. There are ocean currents and strong winds out there. It's no place for any small boat, and I wonder how long the lifeboat will take to get out here too.

"We must put another reef in," yells Felix, "before we hit those waves!"

He turns up into the wind and I press myself against the mast and reef the mainsail, spreading my feet to balance against the rolling swell. I know Felix is right. We'll go slower but we can't risk the bigger sail.

I sit back down in the centerline seat behind Felix as he reefs the jib sail. The wind is stronger, the swell bigger all the time.

We plow into the breaking waves beyond the headland. The first wave runs across the boat, and I take a sharp intake of breath as the water floods across my legs and around my waist. We don't have wet suits or warm gear. It suddenly seems so stupid to have followed Jake out here. I turn to look back, but the land is screened from view behind the rain. Ahead, *Moana* lurches through the waves. I see her buck and jar and slew sideways as the waves knock her off course. We're catching up, despite smaller sails.

Jake and Ethan are struggling. The jib sail is flying loose, and I can see Ethan putting all his weight on the tiller. *Moana* dips and pushes on beyond Gull Rock. They will have to turn her to pass around the other side. I hope they know to sail far beyond Gull Rock before they make the turn. If they try to make the turn too soon, the wind and waves will push them too close to the rocks.

Maybe it's because they're scared to go too far out into the sea, or maybe they misjudge the turn, but Ethan swings *Moana* across the wind, and we see her turn sharply around the rock. Jake is leaning far out on *Moana*'s side, the rope to the mainsail in his hands. I don't have time to yell to Jake. The wind fills the other side of the sail and pushes it across.

The boom swings over, a blur through the air, and I know Jake doesn't stand a chance. His head flies back as he is knocked in a high arc across the sea, his arms flailing above the foaming surf before he disappears beneath the waves.

"Jake!" I scream.

Felix has seen it happen too. He sails toward *Moana*, sailing close behind the cliffs. The sea is in white chaos. The spray from exploding waves showers us like heavy rain. The recoil from the cliff base swamps us with foaming green water and pearl-white surf. The dinghy lurches side to side, her sails almost slap the water.

I push wet hair from my eyes to look for Jake. I hold the mast and rise up on my knees to get a better view. "He's gone!" I yell. "He's gone!"

"We've got to move!" shouts Felix.

We're too close to Gull Rock. If the long centerboard breaks beneath us, we won't stand a chance. I lean out to balance the dinghy as Felix steers toward Ethan and *Moana*. I look back one more time toward Gull Rock. I want to wake up from this nightmare. I can't believe that Jake has gone.

Then I see his head and arms splash above the water. Another wave sweeps over, and he disappears again.

"He's there!" I yell. The waves heave and crest into peaks, curling over near the rocks. Jake's head rises above the water. He claws at the air but sinks under again.

"I see him!" Felix yells.

He swings the dinghy toward Jake. The air is filled with flying sea foam. We ride down one wave into the deep trough and rise up the other side. I look down into the water and see Jake again suspended below us, his shirt billowing around him and his arms outspread as if he's flying underwater.

He's rising toward us through the water. I reach out and grab Jake's shirt as a wave rolls him up, and we fall in a mass of tangled arms and legs inside the boat. For one brief moment I thought I saw a flash of white beneath the waves, something beneath Jake pushing him up toward the air. I look again, but all I see is the white swirl of sea foam in the water.

"Let's get out of here!" Felix yells.

Ethan is clinging to *Moana*'s mast as another wave rolls over her. The sky is black with clouds. There is no horizon. Sea and sky are one. Felix brings the dinghy up on *Moana*'s seaward side. I help Jake pull on a life jacket. He's a deadweight. Blood is pouring through his hair and down his forehead. I grab the other life jacket and scramble across, to join Ethan in Moana.

"Get back to shore," I scream to Felix. "Get Jake back. I'll bring Ethan in *Moana*."

Another wave lifts us and crunches the two boats together. I give the dinghy a shove.

"Just go!" I yell.

Felix pushes the central joystick of his dinghy across and sails away, running with the wind toward the harbor. A gust of wind hits my back and scuds across the ocean. I watch Felix and Jake dissolve into the grainy curtain of rain.

I feel sick and heavy inside. I don't know if I will ever see them again.

36

"Kara!"

Ethan stumbles over to me and clings onto my arm. His face is white. His whole body shakes. He pulls on his life jacket and fumbles with the straps.

Moana heaves and falls over the waves. She's taking on water fast, heeling far over in the water. Another waves spills in the boat, and Ethan and I slip and flounder together while sea foam swirls all around us.

My mind is white with fear. I have to think. I try to think.

A tangle of rope and loose sail spreads across the foredeck into the water. I see now why *Moana*'s heeling in the water. Jake and Ethan have opened the spinnaker sail. It twists under the boat, an underwater parachute, pulling us toward the rocks.

"Help me with this!" I yell. But Ethan doesn't move. He just stands holding the mast, as if he's holding the boat into the sea. I pull and pull on the rope, but the sail is heavy, weighed down into the water. The yawning cliff caves thunder with the breaking waves.

"Ethan," I scream. "The knife. In the locker."

Ethan stumbles forward and pulls stuff from the locker. He finds the short-bladed knife from the toolbox and leans out toward me. I take it in my hands and saw across the spinnaker rope. It cuts loose, and the sail billows away, a monster jellyfish escaping back to sea.

The waves are white-capped mountains now,

vast moving ranges, rising higher and higher. The wind is screaming past, and the air is filled with flying foam. We're being pushed toward the breaking surf. Our only hope now is to sail away. I pull on the mainsail and slide back to the tiller, pulling Ethan with me.

"Stay back here with me!" I yell.

The sail fills with wind, pulls taut, and I feel *Moana* surge forward.

"KARA!" Ethan yells.

I look past him to a wall of dark green water, rising up and up. A freak wave, higher than all the rest.

Everything slows down.

Moana plows up into the wave. She rises up the wave's steep side. But the wave is changing. A crest of foam brims at its peak. *Moana* struggles forward, but the wave is curving inward and begins to break. She can't make it now. *Moana*'s prow twists in the air, and the wave curls over us, folding us in a blanket of green surf. And this moment stays freeze-framed in my mind. *Moana*, on her side, and a thousand tons of water stretched out across us, about to push us down.

I grab Ethan and pull him under one of the seats. *Moana* rolls, and everything goes dark. Seawater rushes in and fills the space we're lying in. The water thunders all around, and through the roar of wind and waves there is a tearing crack, like a gunshot. I can feel it split the water.

Moana spins back up, and Ethan and I burst up for air. *Moana*'s mast is down, ripped apart by rocks beneath the boat. Its jagged end is broken like a stick. But the sail ropes are still attached and anchor *Moana* to the rocks. The sea is boiling all around us. *Moana*'s hull protects us from the full force of the waves. But each wave thumps against her and pushes her toward the cliff. I feel her keel grinding on the rocks below.

"Flares!" I yell. "There's a flare in the front locker."

I scramble forward and reach into the locker. I pull the flare from the clips and try to read the instructions, but *Moana* is heaving in the churning sea. The flare is soaked. I only hope it works. I've never had to use one before. A wave crashes over *Moana*, and I fall back against the hard seat. I pull the tag and hold it skyward. At first nothing happens, but then a blast of light explodes from the flare. I watch its trail spiral upward, and hold there above us, a bright red beacon burning in the darkened skies.

Another wave crushes us against the rocks. One of the metal stays that held the mast rips from the wood and flies close past Ethan's head.

"Get down!" I yell.

Ethan lurches toward me, and we crouch low under the seats. The sound of splintering wood and tearing metal rips through the screaming wind. I feel the hull grind against the rocks below us and know *Moana*'s keel is being wrenched away. It's all that's holding us from being thrown against the cliffs.

311

Ethan and I push farther under the seat as wave
after wave after wave thumps against us. There is
nothing we can do now, nowhere for us to go.
Ethan takes my hand, and I hold his tightly in mine.
The waves thud and thud and thud against *Moana*,
and I can't tell if it's the waves or the hammering of
my heart.

But there's another hammering too, a thudding
high above the waves. A beam of light shines down
and hits the boat.

"HELICOPTER!" Ethan yells.

We scramble out and wave our hands. The beam
holds us fast, and above us a helicopter sways in the
gale.

"We're too close to the cliff!" yells Ethan.

A man drops down toward us, silhouetted by the
light. He drops down on a wire, his feet whizzing
past above our heads. I duck, but Ethan lunges at
his boots. He swings back again and drops into the
boat. He loops a harness over Ethan and grabs me
as a wave swamps over us. We plunge off the side
into the foaming sea. Water rushes into my mouth

and nose. The wire pulls tight, and I feel the lightness of air as the wave passes over, and we rise up above the water. The wind catches us and spins us around and around and around as we lift up into the sky. I look down and see *Moana* far below.

I want to lift her with us too, take her away from here. But as I watch, a wave folds over, lifts her, and she explodes against the cliff. In the spinning kaleidoscope of sea and spray, all that's left of her is twisted metal and flying fragments of splintered wood.

37

"Have you got the others?" I yell.

The winch-man is trying to get me to lie down on a stretcher, but I sit back up. "Have you got them? Have you got Felix and Jake? They went in the other boat."

He speaks into his mouthpiece and holds the headphones tight to his head, so he can hear.

"Where were they heading?"

"To the harbor!" I shout. I feel a pit of fear rise in

me, because he'd have told me if they'd been found.

He speaks again into the mouthpiece, and then the helicopter changes direction, veering sideways.

"We'll take you to the town and get an ambulance for both of you. Then we'll go back out to look for your friends!" he shouts.

I've lost *Moana*, but it feels like nothing to losing Felix and even Jake. Ethan doesn't say anything. He's lying on the stretcher under blankets, eyes closed tight. I wrap my blanket around me and look out beyond the open doorway to the sea below. It's a heaving mass of gray-green surf. I want to see the white sails of Felix's dinghy skimming across the waves below. But rain sweeps across the sky, and we are folded in a cloak of cloud, and it's impossible to see anything out there at all.

My ears pop as we descend onto the playing field outside the town. The sky is black. The streetlights glow dull orange, and cars have their headlights on, even though it's only early evening. The blue light of an ambulance flashes along the top road, coming this way. The winch-man helps us out, guiding us under the turning helicopter blades to the cars parked on the road.

I see Dad running through the rain.

"Kara!" He folds his arms around me and pulls me in. I feel his warm breath in my hair. He holds me tight to him. His whole body shakes and when I look up at him, his face is crumpled into sobs.

"Kara!"

A hand holds me by the shoulder, and I turn to see Felix's mum.

"Where's Felix?" Her hair is plastered to her face and her mascara has run into long black streaks.

Felix's dad and Dougie Evans are there too.

Dougie Evans crouches down beside me. His eyes are wild with fear. "Where's my boy, Kara? Where's my boy?"

The last time I saw Jake, he was stretched across the dinghy, coughing seawater out of his lungs.

"They're in Felix's dinghy," I say, "on their way to harbor."

Lightning flashes across the sky. Felix's mum grasps my arm.

"They could be back by now," I say. It's a wild, impossible thought, but maybe they could. Maybe Felix has got them safely in. "Let's go there," I say.

And it's as if they've been jolted out of sleep.

"Come on," says Felix's dad, "in my car."

Dad wraps me in his coat. "You need a doctor, Kara."

"I'm fine," I say. I pull away and start running after Felix's mum and dad, and we all crowd in the car; Dad, Dougie Evans, and me along the back-seat.

Felix's dad pulls up on the pavement by the harbor, and we spill out and run to the harbor's edge. The flags above the chandlery are flapping hard and the mast lines of the yachts are screaming in the tearing winds. I scan the harbor. All the fishing boats are in, lined up in the deep-water moorings. The yachts and motorboats are secure against the dock. I see the space where *Moana* had once been, and it hits me all over again that she is gone. I won't see her again.

But there is no dinghy in the harbor, no sign of Felix or Jake.

A plume of spray rises over the wall and scatters across a figure looking out to sea. Her black cloak and long hair are flying in the wind. I clamber up on the higher stone ledge next to Miss Penluna. She reaches for my hand, but doesn't take her eyes off the sea.

Felix's mum and dad and Dougie Evans join us, leaning on the granite wall, staring out into the waves. Lightning flashes and a crack of thunder tears the air apart. The tide is high, pushed up farther by the wind and waves. People are lined up all along the wall to watch the storm. It draws people, this sort of power, to see what it can do. Massive waves curl and cross over one another. Foam and spray are flying past.

The helicopter clatters past above our heads.

"They'll find them!" Dad shouts.

But I wonder how, because we can't see anything through the driving rain.

The waves roll in, one after another, massive mountains of moving water, spray flying from the tops like windblown snow. I doubt *Moana* could have sailed in this.

Dougie stands right up on the wall. "MY BOY!" he yells. But the gale flings the words back in his face. "WHERE'S MY BOY?!"

He runs his hands over his head. His eyes are red and wild. He clutches on Dad's arm. "I've lost them, Jim. I've lost both my boys."

Dad puts his arm around him. "Come on. Let's go back and wait for news."

I turn to look at Miss Penluna. She's standing sentrylike, looking out to sea.

Dougie Evans pulls her around to face him. "I want him back."

Miss Penluna stares into his eyes.

"He's all that's left," he sobs.

Miss Penluna pulls her shawl around her. "What

is he coming back to, Dougie? What world are you leaving him?"

Dougie Evans searches her face, and I hear Miss Penluna's words despite the wind and rain. "He's in the company of angels now."

Dougie's knees buckle, and he stumbles to the ground.

A wave slams against the wall, soaking us with freezing spray.

"Come on," says Dad. He pulls my arm.

I look back into the storm one more time.

And it feels as if my heart has skipped a beat, because I saw something, out there. I'm sure I did.

I strain my eyes into the gray veil of rain.

There it is again.

A sail.

A mast and sail rising up behind a wave, and then I see the white hull of Felix's dinghy rear up into sight.

"I SEE THEM!" I yell.

Felix's mum and dad clamber up beside me, and Dougie pulls himself to his feet.

Dougie grabs my shoulder. "Where?"

"There!" I look but the boat has disappeared behind a wall of surf.

It rises up again.

"It's them!" shouts Felix's dad. "It's them."

The boat is so small against these waves. I see Felix in his cockpit seat and Jake slumped in the seat behind.

They are running with the wind. It's on their backs, driving them toward us. They are faster than the waves, outrunning them. The dinghy's bow is well out of the water, and they are skimming across the surface. They dip and ride up another wave. But closer in, the waves are breaking, pounding on the harbor wall. The helicopter clatters through the rain above them. But Felix can't stop now or turn into the wind. They only have one choice, and it looks as if he's chosen it without a second thought. He's heading for the narrow gap between the harbor walls. It seems impossible to aim for in the raging sea.

I glance at Dad, but his eyes are fixed on Felix. Beyond Dad, the crowds along the sea wall are frozen still, just watching. There is nothing anyone can do.

The dinghy is hidden again behind a huge wave. It rides up the back, but the wave is changing, beginning to curl. I want them to miss this wave, let it break without them, but they are past the point of no return, and they slide down the breaking wave, faster and faster, surfing with it, a curling wall of water chasing them in. Too fast, I think, they can't make the narrow gap. The wave is pushing them sideways along the line of breaking surf. Felix throws his weight on the side of the boat. The dinghy's bow swings as the wave crashes over them. I see her mast go down, and all of her is lost in the white foam of the running sea.

The wave explodes against the wall, and I look away. I don't want to see them break against the granite blocks. A foaming wall of surf surges between the harbor walls in a strange and muffled silence. The whole harbor has held its breath, it seems. I clutch Dad and press my head into his chest. But Dad pulls me away.

"Kara, look!"

I look down into the harbor. Through the foaming wall of surf shoots the dinghy. Its sails are shredded and the mast is a wreck of twisted metal. It slews in an arc and comes to rest, rocking gently in the sheltered water. Two figures are slumped inside, motionless.

"FELIX!" I scream.

He leans back in his seat and looks up at me. He gives the thumbs-up and grins. And this time it's a wave of shouts and cheers that explodes all along the harbor walls.

I open my eyes. Through the window, the sky is bright, bright blue. A slight breeze lifts the checked curtain edge, bringing in the salt smell of the sea.

"You've been asleep for ages, Kara."

I turn my head. Daisy is sitting, legs crossed, on her bed, watching me. My neck is stiff, and my body feels heavy. The memories of the day before wash over me.

"What time is it?" I ask.

"It's four o'clock," she says. "You've missed breakfast and lunch, and you've almost missed tea."

I push myself up on my elbows. "It's that late already?"

Daisy nods her head. But her eyes are shining bright, and she's grinning from ear to ear. She climbs down from her bed and takes my arm. "You've got to come with me, Kara," she says. "You've got to come and see."

I swing my legs over the side of the cot. My whole body aches, and my mouth feels dry and sore. I pull on a T-shirt and jeans.

"Come on, there's someone who wants to see you," says Daisy. "She arrived late last night."

"Who?" I ask.

"Surprise," says Daisy. She's at the door, impatient for me to follow. "She's been waiting for you all day."

"I'm coming," I say. I stand up, and the room

spins around me. My head's so thick and heavy, I can hardly think.

Daisy takes my arm again and leads me into her mum and dad's bedroom. Uncle Tom is sitting on the side of the bed, and Aunt Bev is propped up on cushions, her back against the headboard.

Daisy squeezes my hand and grins. "I've got a sister."

And then I see the baby wrapped up in Aunt Bev's arms. She's so small. Eyes closed, lips pouting. Aunt Bev's face is soft and dreamlike. Her hair is loose and tumbles around her shoulders. Her hand is cupped around the baby's head.

Mum must have held me like this once.

"She's beautiful," I say.

Aunt Bev looks up. "Kara," she says, and pats the duvet.

I sit down beside her and just stare at the small baby wrapped in pink.

"Daisy told us what you did yesterday," says Aunt Bev.

I wait for the telling off. I know I shouldn't have left Daisy alone to find Dad.

"You were very brave," Aunt Bev says. I see tears well in her eyes. "But, Kara, you could have *died*."

I reach out to touch the tiny hand that's curled around the blanket's edge.

"You are your mother's child," says Uncle Tom. "It's what she would have done."

I look at them and see something between sorrow and pity in their eyes. The baby's hand grasps my finger, and she squeezes it in her sleep.

"What's she called?" I ask.

Daisy sits down next to me and takes my other hand. She smiles one of her biggest smiles at me. "I chose it," she says. "We've called her Mo, short for Moana. But she'll be just Mo to us."

I feel my eyes burn hot with tears. "Hello, Mo," I say.

I didn't hear Dad come into the room, but when I look up, I see him standing in the doorway.

"Come on," he says. "Let's give them some time

alone. Uncle Tom's going out to sea next week. Dougie Evans gave him back his old job and a pay raise, too."

I look at Uncle Tom, but he's only got eyes for Daisy and Mo.

Dad slips his arm through mine, and I walk with him down the stairs and out into the sunshine. The storm has cleared the air. The colors are brighter, sharper. A car door slams, and Dougie Evans walks up the path, his face hidden behind a huge bunch of flowers. He stops when he sees Dad and me.

"I brought these," he says. "For Bev and the baby."

"Go on up," says Dad.

But Dougie Evans doesn't move. He scrunches the cellophane of the bouquet in his hand.

"How's Jake?" Dad says.

Dougie Evans stares at the floor. "He'll be just fine," he says. "A few stitches on his face, that's all. Might remind him how stupid he was to go out to sea like that."

I try to edge around him, but he's not finished.

He turns to me. "If it weren't for you, my boy would be dead."

I look at Dad and then at Dougie. "It wasn't just me," I mumble.

Dougie scrunches his face into a frown. "Jake said a funny thing too. He said the white dolphin saved him. He said she lifted him up, out of the water."

I watch Dougie Evans wrestle with his thoughts. He twists his hands around and around the stems of the bouquet of flowers. His face is pulled into a tight knot. Pieces of flower stem fall to the floor, but Dougie doesn't seem to notice.

"The truth was staring me in the face all the time," he says. "I just chose not to see it."

Dad puts his hand on Dougie's shoulder. "It's all right, Doug," he says.

But Dougie wants to get this off his chest. "It made me think, it did. That, and what Miss Penluna said. If we go on ripping up the seabed, hauling out all the fish, there'll be nothing left worth saving.

There'll be nothing left for Jake." He clutches the flowers to his chest. "I want you to know, I've signed the petition to stop the dredging. Not just that, but I've signed up to test out new ways of fishing to stop dolphins drowning in our nets too."

I glance at Dad. I can't believe Dougie Evans has changed his mind.

Dad smiles. "Good on you, Dougie."

We turn to walk away, but Dougie calls Dad back and puts out his hand.

"There's a job on one of my trawlers, Jim," he says. "It's yours if you want it."

Dad takes Dougie's hand and shakes it. "Thanks," he says. "But I've got a job lined up already."

I follow Dad down the path and out onto the coastal road along the seafront.

"I don't want to move from here," I say.

Dad smiles and puts his arm around me. "We don't have to," he says. "I didn't find out until yesterday. I didn't want to disappoint you if I didn't get it."

I stop and pull him around to face me. "Get what?" I say.

Dad grins like I've not seen him grin for a long, long time. "I've been accepted on a boat-building course at the boatyard," he says. "I've been assessed, and I'll even have help with my dyslexia. It starts next month."

I wrap my arms around him and hug him tight. "That's brilliant, Dad," I say.

Dad ruffles my hair. "I know. I think so too."

We walk along the road to the far end of the beach and take the path that curls up the hill. I look out to sea, hoping to see a white dorsal fin. I can't get Angel from my mind. She haunts my thoughts now, not my dreams. She's alone out there, without her mother, and I don't know how she will survive all on her own.

"This way," says Dad.

I follow him along the sandy coastal path that runs along the bottom of the campsite fields. "Where are we going?"

"Can't tell you." He smiles. "It's a surprise."

We pass one field of tents to another field of

trailers. The field slopes down to the dunes that back the beach. Beyond the dunes, the sea is calm and silvery blue. It's hard to believe it was a mass of churning green and white last night.

"There," says Dad.

The last trailer faces the sea. Bunting hangs from the trailer across to a line of gorse hedge and dry stone wall. A table is laid with plates and glasses, and a bright pink dolphin windsock is twirling in the breeze. I see shadows in the windows of the trailer. The door bursts open, and Felix tumbles out followed by his mum and dad and Miss Penluna. Carl and Greg and Sam the vet are here, and Chloe and Ella, too.

Dad wraps his arms around me and pulls me close. "Welcome home, Kara," he says.

"Home?" I say. I frown and look at him.

"It's not much, I know, but it's a home for us, for now."

The windows of the trailer face the sea. I'll see and hear the ocean every day. "It's perfect, Dad," I say, and hug him tight. "The best."

Felix pokes me in the ribs. "What kept you?"

I grin. "Where's your medal?"

Felix frowns. "Medal?"

"You won the regatta race, remember?"

Felix laughs. "Yeah, that's right. First the regatta race, next the Olympics."

"Come on," says Felix's dad. "You must all be starving, and we've enough food in the trailer to feed an army."

I smile and look back out across the fields along the stretch of headland. The sunlight slants, golden yellow. It's the first day of September, and the chill of autumn is in the air. I want a moment by myself, just me, before I join them.

"Come on," calls Chloe.

"I won't be long," I say.

I leave them sitting in the sunshine and take the path through the dunes. My toes dig into the cool soft sand. The sea is turquoise, woven through with strands of silver. I climb up onto the highest dune and sit sheltered by the dune grass, and stare out to sea.

"Kara?"

I turn. I hadn't heard Dad follow me. A stream of sand trickles down the dune as he sits beside me. I draw my knees up and fold my arms around them.

"We mustn't be too long," he says. "They've been waiting for you for ages, especially Felix."

I look back at the small white trailer strung with bunting, and the people around the table. I see Felix stretched out on the lounger in the sun. "We've got some good friends, haven't we?"

Dad nods. "If Mum were here, she'd be so proud of you," he says. He scoops up a handful of sand and lets it run through his fingers. "You did what she couldn't do. You made Dougie Evans change his mind."

"Dougie Evans was right, though, wasn't he?" I ask.

Dad turns to me, his eyes crinkled in a smile. "This is Dougie Evans we're talking about, right?"

I frown and fix my eyes on the horizon. "Sometimes the truth does stare us in the face, but we just choose not to look."

Dad sighs and wraps his arm around me. He holds me tight.

I pick a piece of dune grass and twist it in my fingers. "I used to think maybe Mum was too important for us. Maybe she had been chosen for special missions. I thought one day I'd find her in the Amazon jungle saving river dolphins or other animals. I even thought maybe she was an alien from another world, sent to save our planet." My eyes blur with tears despite my smile. "But I know that's not true now."

I feel Dad's arm pull me closer still.

A deep ache knots inside my chest. "We may never know what really happened the night she disappeared," I say. I press my fingers into the sand. "But I know Mum died that night."

I sink my head onto my knees. It feels as if everything I've kept inside is draining out of me, through my fingertips into the cool, cool sand below. "If she had lived, she would have found a way back. She'd be here with us now. She'd be here, because above everything else, she loved us, didn't she?"

I look up at Dad and see his face is wet with tears. I lean into him and stare out to sea. The ocean is flat and calm. Turquoise blue. Small waves crest and run along the shoreline.

"We'll build a new boat, Kara," he says. He wipes the tears from his face. "You and me, we'll build a new boat for us to sail in."

I squeeze Dad's hand and close my eyes. I feel the warm sun on my face. A sea breeze lifts my hair and whispers past me through the dry dune grasses. I hear the curl of surf unfurl along the sand. Above, a seagull cries. I open my eyes and watch it sail across, powder white against a deep blue sky. This whole place feels alive somehow. I feel part of it, as if it's in me too. Maybe this is how Mum felt. Maybe this is how she always knew the dolphins would return. I feel it now. I feel in this moment of deep ocean stillness.

I feel them rising through the water.

"Dolphins!" I yell.

I slide down the dune to the beach and cross the high-tide line of shells and seaweed. My feet slap on the hard wet sand until I am running in the furling waves along the shoreline. I am running alongside the dolphins, their blue-gray bodies arching through the water, the sunlight shining from their smooth wet backs. Their dorsal fins rise and curve above the water, a whole pod of dolphins cruising through the sea.

Then I see her. I see Angel leap from the center. A flash of white, she somersaults in the sunlight and slaps the water with her tail, scattering diamond drops of spray.

"Angel!" I yell.

I wade out beyond the breaking waves.

"Angel!"

She leaps again and I watch her twist and turn before she plunges back into the water. In this golden evening sunlight I feel chosen somehow, as if she's given me the chance to see through into her world.

I know deep down inside, the white dolphin will never be alone.

The vast blue ocean is waiting for her, and this is only the beginning of her story.